Briga-
DOOM

Briga-DOOM

A KATE LONDON MYSTERY

Susan Goodwill

MIDNIGHT INK
WOODBURY, MINNESOTA

First Edition
Second Printing, 2007

Book design by Donna Burch
Cover design by Kevin R. Brown
Cover illustration © 2006 by Kim Johnson/Lindgren & Smith

Midnight Ink, an imprint of Llewellyn Publications

Library of Congress Cataloging-in-Publication Data

Goodwill, Susan.
 Briga-doom : a Kate London mystery / Susan Goodwill. — 1st ed.
 p cm.
 ISBN 13: 978-07387-1037-2
 ISBN 10: 0-7387-1037-7
 1. Divorced women—Fiction. I. Title.

PS3607.O59226B75   2007
13'.6—dc28   2006046886

Midnight Ink
Llewellyn Publications
2143 Wooddale Drive, Dept. 0-7387-1037-7
Woodbury, MN 55125-2989, U.S.A.
www.midnightinkbooks.com

Printed in the United States of America

For *Mom*,
I'll meet you under 'G' in that big library in the sky.

ONE

"You look ridiculous, Kate," my Aunt Kitty said.

This coming from a seventy-four-year-old in a black-feathered turban, yellow dance leotard, blue high-tops, and red plaid mini-skirt.

I sighed and closed the door behind her. I felt ridiculous. Golf clothing was new to me, pink was not my color, and the socks, with their little pom-poms bouncing around my ankles, made me feel like the rear window of a Chevy low-rider.

Kitty and I stood in the lobby of the London family's dubious legacy, the Egyptian Theatre. She handed me a Styrofoam coffee cup.

"The outfit's for Ronnie's golf outing," I said. "He picked it out."

"Well, darling, you can always divorce him," she said, maneuvering her way across the loose floor tiles behind me. "They'll get easier now that you've gone through one. By your third or fourth, you'll slide through like a hot knife through butter."

1

"Can we at least wait until I marry this guy?" I set my coffee on the glass top of the dusty concession stand. *If. If I marry him.*

"Details." Kitty waved her hand and blew at the top of the counter, sending a cloud of plaster dust into the air between us. She plunked down her zebra-striped tote bag and her coffee cup.

I eyed the skimpy pleated skirt surrounding her middle. "Is that a kilt?"

"It's for *Brigadoon*—my own version of method acting." Kitty smiled her semi-famous, former-movie-star smile and raised a scrawny arm over her head. Her feathery headgear flapped as she shuffled her high-tops in an abbreviated Highland Fling. "Look out, world. The Mudd Lake Players are back to break a few more legs."

She beamed that thousand-watt grin at me, waiting.

"They're ba-ack!" I said, but I sounded like the girl from *Poltergeist.* I tried again. "Look out, world!"

Once you threw in the Mudd Lake Players, our dubious legacy became a full-fledged family curse.

A narrow shaft of sunlight flashed through the dust motes in the air between us. I looked up at a jagged opening in the ornate plaster. "I swear to God, this place has a terminal disease. That hole wasn't there yesterday."

Kitty leaned her head back and squinted at the ceiling. "At least it matches all the others," she said. "No worries, luv. The Grand Marquis'll be here at ten. He'll patch us up in plenty of time for next month's show."

The Grand Marquis, aka Morris Hirschberger, was not royalty; he was Kitty's fourth ex-husband out of seven. He drove a Grand

Marquis. She had trouble keeping all their names straight, but she never forgot their cars.

Her last few words hit me, and I felt my eyes go wide. "Did you say next month? We aren't due to open for three months . . . at least."

"I've been meaning to tell you. I've consulted with my astrologer, and Roland swears all the planets and houses and whatnot will be aligned precisely on my birthday. Can you believe it? We've been rehearsing at the Senior Center."

Kitty reached in her tote bag and pulled out the local paper, the *Mudd Lake Eavesdropper*. She held it up so that I could see the back of section one.

"Surprise!" she said.

A full-page ad trumpeted the news:

LERNER AND LOEWE'S
Brigadoon

At the Egyptian Theatre
Grand Reopening October 10!

October tenth, Kitty's seventy-fifth birthday, was a month from today. A month? A pounding headache stomped into the space behind my eyeballs.

"Kitty, there's just no way—"

A loud crash, followed by clattering, cut me off. I trotted to the first set of doors that led to the main theatre and squinted through the dim light from the doorway.

Down on the stage the curtain moved. There was no wind in the theatre. And there were supposed to be no people. I froze.

Faint scuffling and then a tearing sound came from behind the curtain. The fabric moved again.

I reached around the corner and pulled a club out of my brand-new golf bag. Clutching it, I stepped into the auditorium.

"Hey," I tried to make my voice deep, "who's down there?"

Kitty was right behind me.

"There's somebody in the theatre," I whispered, "probably kids."

She shoved her way up beside me. "Perhaps it's the Naked Bandit. Let me see!"

I kind of wanted to see the Naked Bandit myself. Word had it he snatched women's purses wearing only a ski mask and Adidas. I held Kitty back with one hand.

"Stay here," I told her and jogged down the aisle toward the stage. "You'd better be gone by the time I get there," I yelled. I brandished my seven-iron in the direction of the curtain. "I'm armed."

I stopped midway down the aisle and listened.

"If you're the Naked Bandit," Kitty trilled, "hang on a second. I've got my camera in my bag. Don't leave."

Head feathers flapping, she trotted toward the lobby.

A clatter came from behind the curtain. "Shit!" said a muffled voice. More clattering, then "Ouch!"

A figure emerged from behind the blue velvet and ran down the stairs at stage left. I let out an involuntary yelp, and my heart started doing Tae Bo kicks. I turned to run back up the aisle and almost ran over Kitty.

She held her digital camera up to her face. "Say cheese, darling!" The camera flashed in the dim light.

Nobody breathed for a few seconds, then the emergency door flew open and sunshine glared from outside. The figure wasn't naked. It was clothed from head to toe in a hooded monk's robe. I couldn't be sure, but from the back it looked like Obi-Wan Kenobi.

* * *

"Yes, that's Obi-Wan," Kitty said. "I'm certain of it."

We were back at the doorway to the auditorium, examining the digital photo on her camera.

"That outfit's from our costume rack, from the Mudd Lake Players' *The Star Wars Monologues*," Kitty said. "What a stinker that was."

There was no arguing that point.

"There's no way to tell who this is," I said. "It could be anybody."

"And, if he's naked under there, you'd never prove it by me." Kitty peered at the display. "Darn it all."

"Flip on the lights, and I'll go see if there's any damage." I started back inside, grabbing my seven-iron again just in case.

Kitty switched on the houselights, and the huge art deco chandelier above the seating area came to life. I looked up. Kitty's father had ordered that chandelier from Vienna in 1926. When I was little she told me it came from an enchanted castle—a part of me still bought it. When I'd come to Kitty a bewildered little five-year-old, shattered and alone, she'd used this theatre, this magical place built by her parents, to put me back together again, to bring me back to life. Now, restoring the Egyptian was my chance to return the favor. The headache marched back with reinforcements. *A month*?

"Would you like me to call the sheriff?" Kitty asked.

My stomach did a somersault. "Nope." I headed for the wide staircase to the balcony.

I checked the seating area, then jogged back downstairs and peeked into the control booth—no signs of damage. I walked down the side aisle to the emergency exit and shoved the push bar. The steel door swung wide and slammed against the brick wall of the building. The lock had been pried apart.

I stuck my head into the narrow alley. Deserted. The wooden stairs that led up to my apartment were empty, and the steel door at the top remained untouched. Ernie was up there, and woe to the Naked Bandit who met up with my little dog.

I grabbed a rope from the wings and used it to tie the exit door shut, then I headed backstage. Aside from a few toppled scenery cutouts, everything looked untouched.

Kitty stood at the back of the theatre while I walked up front and pulled the rope that opened the huge velvet house curtain.

"Good Godfreys!" Kitty said, and under her breath, "Holey tamoley!"

I swiveled to her, saw shock on her face, and turned back. Streaks of red spray paint marred the stage floor. Cans of scenery colors lay on their sides. That must've been the clattering. One of the lids had come off a paint can and thick baby-blue latex formed a puddle across the boards.

It was then that I saw the backdrop: the idyllic Scottish hillsides cloaked in mist that I'd spent every night for the last two weeks painting. I stood for several seconds while my heart snaked its way into my shoes and tightness gripped my throat. Material hung down to the floor from deep gashes. Spray-painted obscenities covered what fabric remained on the frame: mostly references to female body parts, the oldest profession, and non-missionary-style sexual positions.

Yikes.

Kitty walked down the main aisle and stood in front of the stage.

"My heavens." She held her hand over her chest, turned her head sideways, and read the obscenities. She pointed to a word. "I don't believe I've tried that one since the sixties."

I turned back to the stage and ran my finger down a slice in the canvas.

This wasn't a kid, and I guessed it wasn't the Naked Bandit either. The angry gashes and choice of words made me think this guy'd do more to women than snatch purses with a pink plastic squirt gun. And he had a knife. Suddenly, I was very glad I'd stopped halfway down the aisle.

TWO

I DIDN'T WANT KITTY alone in the theatre so we cancelled the Grand Marquis, then I dropped her at the Senior Center for yoga. I wanted to grab a fried-egg sandwich at Mama's Deli but there wasn't time, so I drove toward Bramblewood Hills on the outskirts of town.

To get the Egyptian open in three months would take a minor miracle; a little over four weeks would take downright divine intervention—especially after the damage this morning. Plus, I was hungry, I was crabby, and I didn't have a clue how to play golf.

I drove under the *Buy Rite Real Estate, Where Everybody Goes Home Smiling* banner and parked my car. I slipped off my Puma Speedcats and tied the laces on my brand-new, clunky golf shoes with the little plastic points on the bottom—a gift from Ronnie. I frowned down at my feet. They looked fat and unattractive.

Now, I'm no fashionista, and, I admit, I wear a lot of jeans and black sweaters, but I have a Thing about My Shoes. Life is too short to wear the ugly ones, or to pay full price for that matter. If

I planned to keep golfing, I'd have to go online and shop. Surely I could find a close-out on these things—at Prada, maybe?

My spikes clicked on the pavement as I walked up to the kiosk to register. Lance Beaton, Buy Rite's office manager, stepped to the counter and stood next to me—very much next to me. I took two steps to the side.

The crisp fall sunshine glared and flashed off Lance's synthetic shirt, a shiny Lycra number that featured fifties couples bowling. A carpal tunnel brace surrounded Lance's right wrist. Today's look aimed for Retro Chic, but he'd missed and touched down on Fashion Refugee.

Lance winced as he lifted green flip-up sunglasses. He squinted at me and moved closer. "I s-s-saw the paper. Wh-wh-when are the t-t-tryouts for *Br-r-rigadoon*?"

I took a step back. "Sorry, Lance. *Brigadoon*'s already cast and in rehearsals. The Mudd Lake Players are doing the whole thing."

"Ohhh, n-n-n-no."

I knew just what he meant.

"M-m-maybe I should j-j-join the Players." He eyed me up and down and began breathing through his mouth.

I folded my arms across my chest and resisted the urge to squirm. He handed me a black Buy Rite hat with its white smiley-faced house logo and shuffled closer.

"Thanks," I said. I sidled further away. "Um, what do I do?"

Lance slid his eyes away from my chest and consulted a clipboard. "Y-y-you're on eighteen," he said and pointed toward the collection of golf carts at the back of the clubhouse.

I could feel him watching as I clacked around the building.

The golf pro strapped my clubs into a golf cart, a silent, electric model.

I hopped in, and using the little map on the back of the scorecard, followed the pro's directions to the eighteenth tee. Maybe golf would cheer me up. My buggy purred along. I was outside and not selling real estate. The birds were chirping; the sky was that crystalline blue that only happens on a sunny Michigan autumn morning. Plus, I was engaged to the perfect man.

I knew he was perfect—successful, attentive, responsible, charisma up the wazoo. I said a quick prayer to the God of Second Chances, "Please God, help me out. All I have to do is set a date."

I heard a cell phone chirp, and that's when I saw them.

My cart was so quiet, we were almost a ménage a trois before the couple in the bushes even noticed me.

"Ronnie?"

I jammed hard on the brakes and jerked to a stop. My fiancé, Mayor Ronnie Balfours, and his real estate client, Estelle Douglas, rustled around in the shrubs at the edge of the path to the seventeenth hole. At first, I thought the two of them were searching for a lost ball, but upon closer inspection, I realized the only searching they'd been doing was on each other. They looked up, two shifty-eyed deer caught in my headlights.

"Kate! Oh Jeeze. Kate. We were, uh . . ."

Ronnie shoved and tugged at his clothing, trying to stuff everything back where it belonged.

"Woops!" Estelle's cell phone chirped again. She put it to her ear as she began climbing upward through the shrubs and brambles.

"I was just leaving," she called over her shoulder. "Sorry, Kate."

She acted more like she'd just borrowed my putter, not taken her own personal PGA tour of my betrothed's body. Ronnie climbed down and stood on the blacktopped path directly in front of me.

Big mistake.

His normally neat blonde hair stuck out in random clumps all over his head.

"Kate?"

I glared at him. "Ronnie, I cannot believe this. You rotten . . . you cheating . . . you . . ."

There wasn't a word bad enough for how I felt about him. I banged the steering wheel and growled in frustration.

Ronnie started toward my cart, then he must've caught a good look at my eyes because he stopped dead and began backing away.

"Let's not get emotional here, Kate. I'm Mr. Right. Remember? You said so yourself." He shoved his lavender golf shirt down into his belt; it hung out on one side. "I'm still perfect for you."

Uh-huh. Now I knew why every time I tried to set a date, I felt like I did when I tried on a pair of $100 size seven shoes marked down to ten bucks . . . I wear an eight.

I pressed my size eight toward the floor, and the golf cart nosed forward.

"Kate, wait—This is my golf outing, for cripes' sakes. Our clients . . . my voters . . . Let's reason this out . . . This is just a little— this doesn't matter." He was backing away faster now.

I thought about how Ronnie had pushed me to set a wedding date. How I'd pushed myself. My stomach rolled itself into a fist-sized knot.

"Hey, Ronnie, guess what?" I yelled. "You can't be Mr. Right without fidelity. Fidelity matters. It matters a hell of a lot!" I sped up. I'd never driven a golf cart before. It was easier than I thought.

Ronnie turned and broke into a trot, stuffing again at his shirt. "Kate, it was a mistake. Anyone can make a mistake." He tossed the words over his shoulder as he picked up speed.

"Mistake? You call that a mistake? Mashing Estelle Douglas is not a mistake, Ronnie. Spectacularly stupid, but not a mistake." I lobbed a golf ball at his head. I missed; maybe if I'd taken lessons.

I finally found a good word for him.

"Ronnie, you bastard!" I yelled. My voice echoed through the valley. Other golfers got out of their carts: men in plaid pants, women in unflattering Buy Rite golf hats. They all peered in our direction.

Ronnie looked desperately from side to side. A steep, brambly hill rose to his right, and the ground dropped off to his left. He stayed on the path.

"Sweetie . . . shhh . . . my vote—your clients," he climbed the incline toward the crest of the hill.

"Don't you sweetie me." Those golf carts don't go fast enough. I tried lifting my foot and jamming it down again.

We were almost to the eighteenth green. Ronnie was running now. "Kate, calm down . . . Kate, stop it . . . Help!"

Four port-o-johns were lined up, obedient soldiers at the crest of the hill. The sun peeked out from behind them. It glinted off their shiny metal door frames and glowed through their green plastic walls.

The hill steepened, and my buggy hesitated a bit from the effort. Ronnie gulped up a second wind and ducked into the end port-o-john.

So. I ask you.

What's a girl to do?

I sat there a second or two while my whole future, my whole new life, slithered down the drain.

Well, to Hell with Mr. Right. To Hell with Buy Rite Real Estate. To Hell with it all.

I jammed my foot to the floor.

The cart jerked forward, and I slammed full force into Ronnie's port-o-john. There was a resounding "crack" as metal hit plastic, and the impact rocked my head forward. The sound soared through the fall sunshine and sang over the makeshift village of waiting golfers.

I froze. The potty teetered tentatively for a moment. Then, all at once it lurched over on its back like a prom queen in stilettos. A satisfying smack and a small whooshing sound spilled out. The toilet emitted a huge slosh, a gurgle, and a few rumbles. It launched itself and sledded down the grassy hill, gaining momentum as it went. From its bowels spewed a long, loud, and exceptionally flamboyant stream of swear words.

Ronnie'd always had the gift. Words I'd never even think of, he'd put together.

"Uh-oh," I muttered.

Toboggan Alley, we used to call that slope when we were kids. I got out of the cart and looked over at the clusters of people that stood on the surrounding hills. Some held their hands to their mouths in horror; a few started to snicker. Everyone peered into the sun-drenched valley.

Thanks to the natural amphitheater formed by Bramblewood's sloping terrain, there wasn't a bad view in the house. The entire course witnessed Ronnie Balfours, our mayor, my boss and ex-fiancé, climb out of the capsized port-o-potty. He looked a lot like a cosmonaut, emerging from his little green space capsule in the middle of the fairway, or perhaps more like an alien, since he was dripping with slimy blue antiseptic from head to toe.

"Kate, you bitch!" he yelled. "You're fired. Your theatre's history! Somebody call the police."

THREE

THE GOLF PRO CHUGGED up the path behind me. He hopped out and stalked to my side. I watched his bushy eyebrows form one angry line under his complimentary Buy Rite golf hat.

"I can just drive it back," I said. I gave him a "trust-me" kind of look.

He returned it with a look that screamed "I wouldn't trust you with roller skates." He yanked the keys out of my slightly cracked but still drivable golf cart.

"We'll just leave it here for the sheriff," he said.

My heart began to pound: the sheriff.

He then escorted me back to the clubhouse—in his cart.

I ducked into the ladies' room and splashed ice-cold water on my overheated face. I wondered if it was possible to live in here. I could order in food, wash in the sink. I tried what I assumed was a yoga breath—I was never trained in yoga either.

A minute or two later, the pro rapped on the door. "C'mon. He's waiting for you."

I got halfway out, went back to the mirror, ran my fingers through my sweaty auburn curls, and swiped on some lipstick. I hadn't seen Ben since our breakup over fifteen years ago. I'd known the guy since we were five. Now I got to see him for the first time again, and, oh joy, I got to look like a complete idiot. If I had to look like an idiot, at least I'd look like an idiot with Tawny Surprise lips. I pulled open the bathroom door, brushed past the golf pro, and stepped out into the parking lot.

And there he was.

He looked the same as when he'd left for dental school, except his shoulders were wider. He still had the full head of dark hair and the same great hips, the ones that got me into regular trouble in the back seat of his Camaro from my seventeenth birthday until halfway through Kalamazoo College. The sun reflected in flashes off his Elk County sheriff's badge and sunglasses.

"Hi, Ben." My heart skipped around in my chest. "This is just so silly." I tried to smile; it came out as a twitchy muscle spasm. "It was just a—I lost my temper. It was just a thing, a . . ." I dove for a sane explanation for my behavior, something that would get me out of this mess. I came up dry. "A—lost temper thing—an accident, really." I patted thin air with my hand. "We should just forget about it. I promise, I'll never golf again."

He was taking in everything, my black *Buy Rite Real Estate, Where Everyone Goes Home Smiling* hat, my pink golf shirt, my pink madras shorts. I watched as his mirrored lenses came to rest on the pink pompoms ringing my ankles and on the shoes.

One corner of his mouth curled up, and the dimple I thought of more than I cared to admit appeared.

I faced twin reflections of myself as he looked up.

"I heard you were back," he said. "Surprised we didn't run into each other until now." He unhooked handcuffs from their place on his belt. "You look good, Kate. It looks like you've been flossing. Now, turn around."

I had a flash of memory back to when we were little kids on Elm Street. I would wear my tin sheriff's badge and use my plastic handcuffs to arrest Ben and lock him in his parents' garage. In return, I would have to sit in a lawn chair while Ben pretended to drill my teeth with his father's DeWalt.

Now, half of Mudd Lake's adult population watched as Ben Williamson fastened my hands behind my back. These handcuffs were real, and they pinched.

I tried shifting my wrists around.

Ben leaned close to my ear, and I felt his breath as he whispered, "Sorry."

He took his finger, placed it in the center of the cuffs, and gave them a little shake. They loosened a bit.

I scanned the crowd and spotted Charlene Lebonowitz standing in a cluster of people at the end of the parking lot. She looked sweaty and flushed in her orange jogging suit with fall leaves appliquéd over the chest. She'd never golfed either.

Charlene is my best friend, and I never thought I'd say this, but thank God she's an attorney. I looked her in the eye and mouthed the word: "Help."

Charlene started across the parking lot.

"Maybe we could sort this out without . . . going anywhere?" I said over my shoulder.

Ben leaned in a bit. "Nope. Sorry."

I felt his breath again brushing across the top of my ear, plus heat radiated from his chest warming my back. Unlike Ronnie, who reeked of Polo cologne, Ben smelled like soap and fresh air. Even after all these years, there was a familiar sexuality about him. I leaned back. I caught myself and jerked upright.

Yikes! Post-romantic stress disorder was making me a crazy woman.

I bent forward. I promised myself to go right back to avoiding Ben Williamson—as soon as I got out of these handcuffs.

I swiveled my head and looked at him out of the corners of my eyes. "I have a lawyer," I said.

"I see her." He lifted his head and called out across the crowd, "Charlene, meet us at the Oscenada jail, okay?"

Oh, the joys of small-town living.

Ben deposited me behind the mesh-screened divider of his SUV, belted me in, and pulled out of the parking lot.

I watched glimpses of Lake Michigan roll by, serene and blue. It sparkled in the distance as we headed out on the highway toward the next county and the jail.

I rehearsed the question I'd had for Ben Williamson for about a decade and a half. I screwed up my courage and leaned my head forward.

"Ben?"

His radio squawked. He unclipped it from its holder and clicked a button.

"Williamson, here."

The dispatcher's voice sounded tinny. "Sheriff Williamson, we need you out at the plaza across from the Wal-Mart, right away."

"If you want me to pick up your prescription again, Eunice, I'm busy. I'm bringing somebody in on assault."

Assault?

"No boss, it's real serious. There's a dead body out there. Stabbed."

Ben hesitated. "Did you say stabbed? As in murder?"

"It looks that way. A witness saw someone bent over the body. The suspect fled the scene on foot."

"I'm on it," he said and clicked off his radio. He flipped a few switches and without turning around, said, "Hang on."

"With what?" I yelled over the beginning wail of the siren.

Red and blue flashes strobed across the hood, and the siren howled to life. Ben whipped the steering wheel. With my hands locked behind me, I rocked first right, then left, and bounced back to an upright position. We jostled our way across the median, then slammed out onto the highway skidding tires and spewing gravel. My head jerked back and plastered itself into the headrest.

We screamed past Mudd Lake on the bypass highway and crossed the bridge at the edge of town. A few minutes later, we skidded into Medication Nation Plaza and swerved through the parking lot, barely missing a red Mercedes and a Domino's Pizza delivery car. I bounced back and forth again and ended up tilted sideways to the left as we careened around the corner of the building. I sprang back to vertical, and my head rocked forward as we screeched to a halt.

Ben flicked off the siren but left the flashers on. I craned my head to see and was instantly glad I hadn't grabbed that fried-egg sandwich.

A young man's body lay sprawled on the asphalt. White-blond spikes poked out all over the man's head, as in very pointy hair. And in the man's back stuck a shiny, no doubt very pointy, knife.

FOUR

BEN OPENED HIS CAR door and walked to the body. He knelt down and felt the neck for a pulse. After a few seconds, he shook his head and came back to the car.

He stood outside the door, reached in, and grabbed the radio. He clicked it on.

"Eunice, this guy's still warm."

I'd only done dead at Leo Plotsky's Haven of Mortuary Peace and Discount Granite Supply. Dead at Leo's was powdered and fluffed, and it definitely wasn't warm.

Little clear dots slid down in front of my eyeballs. I tried to put my head down, but the restraint held fast. I shoved my chin against my chest.

Through the blood rushing in my ears, I heard Ben ask for backup. Eunice's voice crackled from the radio. "The closest state police unit they have is thirty minutes away."

"Tell them to hurry," Ben said. "Who am I looking for?"

"Girl's name's LaDonna MacRae."

21

Ben's voice was grim. "I know her. I arrested the dead guy for assaulting her a month ago."

He stood a second, looking over the door at the body. A lone rusty blue hatchback hunched behind it. The word "bitch" stood out in angry red spray paint across the hood.

Ben leaned his head in through the door toward me. "That's LaDonna's car," he said. "Guess what. You get to be a deputy."

"*What?*" I squeaked. I'd meant to sound indignant, but I was too busy holding down my empty stomach.

He walked around the car and undid my restraint. He reached behind me, unlocked my handcuffs, and snapped them to his belt. "You don't look so good," he said.

I swallowed, put my head between my knees.

"Sit a sec," Ben said. "You still get the hiccups?"

I nodded, holding my breath.

"Keep breathing."

He rummaged around in the back of the Tahoe while I took deep breaths with my face aimed between my legs. In a few seconds he was back, standing outside my open door. I lifted my head.

He handed me a roll of yellow tape. It said, SHERIFF'S LINE DO NOT CROSS.

"Do you have a cell phone?" he asked.

My purse was on the front seat of the Tahoe.

I pointed. "Yeah, in there."

He pulled it out and scrawled his number on a piece of paper. He handed both items to me.

"Kate, I need you to get out of the car," he said.

My legs felt rubbery as I climbed out. I took a few clacking steps, stopped, and looked down. I'd forgotten I was wearing golf shoes.

"I can't have gawkers contaminating this crime scene," Ben said.

Behind him, by the freight entrance to Medication Nation, a teenaged kid with multiple lip rings and green hair huddled with an older woman. They stared in our direction through a cloud of cigarette smoke.

Ben pointed to the light poles closest to the car and the body. "Run this tape around these and over to the poles by Interior Beauty and BatCave Music. Don't let anyone inside but the state police. I'm going to check out the area. I'll be back in five."

He jumped into the Tahoe and backed up. The window slid down, and he stuck his head out.

"Call me if you see a black-haired girl, about five-eleven. Looks like she's dressed for Halloween. She might try to get back to her car," he said. He did a U-turn and drove out of the lot.

The killer could still be here? I hiccupped. I didn't want to be a deputy! I dropped the tape. I let out an involuntary "Oops," and stooped to get it. It bumped on the ground and rolled away.

It unfurled toward the body and bounced over the corpse's outstretched hand. I cringed. The roll disappeared into the dense bushes at the back of the lot. It laid down a trail of black and yellow DO NOT CROSSes behind it.

I clacked after it, hiccupping. I followed the roll through the shrubs, pushing pungent evergreen branches out of my face and ducking red-tinged sumac. I wondered, was the red stuff at the top poisonous? I didn't touch it, just in case.

The terrain sloped gently behind the lot. The roll kept ahead of me by wheeling under the shrubs just out of reach. Skirting a sumac, I followed the DO NOT CROSSes to a point where the brush fell away to a steep, wooded embankment. The roll collided with a tree root and toppled to its side. I bent down and grabbed it.

"Gotcha," I said and hiccupped.

Halfway down the embankment, a flash of dark hair and black clothing moved through the trees.

My heart pole-vaulted in my chest. I held very still and looked for more movement. Nothing.

Holding my breath, I backed carefully away from the edge. Then I scrambled up the slope as silently as I could, given my foot-gear. I tiptoed across the asphalt of the parking lot, dragging and rolling the tape as I went.

"Come on. Come on." With shaky hands, I punched in Ben's number.

"She's here," I whispered.

"What do you mean, she's here?" he said.

"I just saw her. She's down the hill behind the parking lot." I pointed as if he could see me.

There was the briefest of pauses. "What were you doing down—?"

I cut him off, "Just get back here, okay?" I hiccupped again.

My heart whacked against my rib cage, and every few seconds, I hiccupped. I didn't know what else to do, so I clicked and scritched around the lot. I wrapped the light poles and pulled the tape tight. I encircled the body and the potential getaway car.

I'd just finished when Ben pulled into the lot. He leapt out and grabbed my arm.

"Show me where," he said and pulled me toward the shrubs.

"She might be dangerous." I dug my spikes in. They scratched over the pavement as he tugged. "She might have a gun—"

"Kate, I know her. I help out at the free clinic, and I've seen her there since she was seven. Besides, if she had a gun, she would've used it already." He jerked his head at the skewered Mohawk-person ringed in crime scene tape and continued pulling me.

I led him to the edge of the embankment and pointed. Ben unsnapped his holster. He worked his way down the steep hill while I followed. I used my spikes to grip the soft earth. With my heart thudding so hard against my chest it almost knocked me off balance, I stood behind him and held my breath.

"LaDonna?" he said.

There was no sound.

He made his voice soothing. "Come on, LaDonna."

Ben looked in all directions.

He called into the trees, "Running'll only make it worse. You won't get far. You know it. Think of your mom."

There was a snort from behind a stand of sumacs. We both looked at the shrubs.

"Okay, sorry," Ben said. "Think of your cat, then."

The bushes moved and from twelve or fifteen feet away, a young vampire stood up. At least that's what she looked like to me. Owlish black circles surrounded her eyes. Her unnaturally black hair gave her pale skin the same greenish tint as a glow-in-the-dark Jesus.

The vampire started to cry. Through her tears she said, "I didn't do it. I didn't kill Taz Dixon."

"Okay, okay," Ben said. "It's okay. We'll sort this out. We'll help you through it."

The girl began to sob.

Ben worked his way through the brush to the wailing girl and took her arm. He led her slowly back to the path. It was then I noticed that she wore a cast on her left foot. I also noticed that her right hand was covered in blood.

"You're going to have to help her up the hill," Ben said.

"Me?" I backed up three steps. "Why can't you do it?"

"Because somebody has to hold the gun."

I stared at him and hiccupped.

"If I cuff her, she can't climb the hill," Ben said. "I can't let her use me as support, not while I'm armed. It has to be you."

I put my hands on my hips. "What if I say no?"

The girl continued to bawl uncontrollably.

Ben pulled out his gun. "I'll shoot you," he said.

The girl wailed and went back to gulping out sobs.

I glared at him, my hands still on my hips. "Go ahead." I hiccupped, turned, and took two scratchy steps up the embankment. "It could only help."

"Kate, I'm kidding," Ben said to my back. "Please come back here, okay?"

I sighed and turned around. "What do I need to do?"

Ben had me pat the sides of LaDonna's long black skirt, then her top. Buckles hung across the back of her shirt near the shoulders and odd rings stuck out from the sleeves. I'm no expert so I couldn't be sure, but it looked like a straitjacket dyed black, with the sleeves shortened. The girl heaved out sobs through the entire procedure.

"Is that barbed wire?" I said, pointing to LaDonna's neck.

LaDonna touched her throat and, between big, wet sniffles, spoke her first semi-coherent word. It sounded like "Dadoo."

I looked at her. "What?"

She sniffled. "It's a tattoo."

Ben still held the gun but pointed up at the sky. Using his free hand, he gestured to me. "Kate, get beside her, and let her put her arm over your shoulder."

I glared at him some more. He rolled his gun in the air. "Let's go."

I took a few hesitant steps and tried to quell my panic. On tiptoe I'm a little over five-six, and LaDonna stood almost a head taller. She put her arm over my shoulder, enshrouding me in a cloud of musky patchouli.

She held her bloody hand away from my shirt and sniffled some more. "Thanks," she said.

LaDonna leaned into me as we climbed up the hill. Ben followed less than an arm's length behind.

As soon as we reached the top of the embankment, Ben took LaDonna's arm and led her across the lot. I followed.

He cuffed her and belted her into the back of the Tahoe. I stepped close to him and turned my back to the car.

"That was terrible! I can't believe you did that to me. Plus, I'm not comfortable riding back there with her," I whispered. Panic skittered over me in another chilly wave. "In case you hadn't noticed, she's probably a murderer."

"Believe me, I would've been on top of her if she so much as twitched." He looked at LaDonna, who was attempting to wipe her nose on the shoulder of her straitjacket. "About the car, yes, you have a point. You can ride up front."

A state police car pulled into the lot.

"I need to talk to them and get a statement from the witness," he said. "By the way, you're no longer a deputy. You're under arrest again."

I rolled my eyes.

He held the passenger door open for me. I got in, and he shut it, took his glasses off, and tossed them through the window past my lap. Then he winked at me.

I sucked in a quick gasp of air. God, those eyes . . . I'd forgotten. My body parts lit up like a pinball machine. I focused on staying mad at Ben, on hating men in general. It didn't work.

A lot of sniffling was coming from the back seat. I faced forward but my throat tightened in sympathy.

The sniffling subsided a bit. "You a deputy?" a small voice said.

I turned in my seat. "Yep."

LaDonna craned her neck up high and looked at me. "Weird outfit," she said. "You undercover?"

I glanced down at my pink pom-poms and then turned my head toward the back. "Yep," I said.

"You're gonna help me, right?" she said. "Because I think I'm being framed."

At that moment Ben pulled open the car door. We drove on to the jail.

FIVE

CHARLENE STOOD WAITING IN the lobby of the Oscenada County Building.

"What took you guys so long?" she said to Ben. She eyed LaDonna.

"Oh," she said.

Ben spoke quietly to Charlene, then pulled LaDonna away in the direction of the jail cells.

"I don't have to stay here, do I?" I asked Charlene.

"No . . . I hope not. We have a date with a judge. Ronnie isn't too well-liked out here, and that's in our favor," she whispered.

We made our way down the hall.

We stood outside a judge's chambers: Helen Reed, it said on the door.

I stopped, but Charlene grabbed my arm, dug in her pink acrylic nails, and pulled me into the room. Judge Reed sat behind a large mahogany desk. She was good-looking, in her late fifties or early sixties, and dressed, not in judge's robes, but in a sharply tailored gray wool suit.

Still golf shod and clacking along like a Clydesdale, I felt, looked, and sounded like an absolute idiot. For Charlene's purposes, ideal.

Charlene argued eloquently, talking about mental duress and breach of promise, mitigating circumstances, and a badly installed port-o-potty.

Judge Reed dropped my assault charges provided I attended six months of anger management classes. If I didn't attend class or knocked over any more port-o-potties, I'd be sentenced to something nastier.

"We'll get a chance to see how serious you are right away. Dr. Alice Parker has a new class starting tomorrow at the junior high school gym. Be there at noon."

Charlene raised an eyebrow. "She's back?"

Judge Reed smiled and folded her arms over her chest. She nodded. "Uh-huh."

Judge Reed and Charlene exchanged a look.

"Oh boy," Charlene said.

The judge grinned at Charlene and signed a paper. She handed it to Charlene and nodded in the direction of the cellblock. "It beats what's in second place."

We stood in the hall outside Judge Reed's office. "What was that all about?" I asked.

"Nothing. She was pretty easy on you. Anger management class is the lightest thing she could give you, considering Ronnie's the mayor." She grinned. "You're in for a treat. Dr. Al is . . . unique."

"Okay." I could do anger management class. I'd go for my PhD if it'd keep me out of the hoosegow.

As we walked out into the clear fall afternoon, Charlene told me Her Honor's husband had left her for a twenty-three-year-old lap dancer.

She grinned at me. "She probably wishes you'd take her husband golfing."

"Ha ha. I'm never golfing again."

Marci, Charlene's paralegal, had driven my Riviera to the jail. We stood next to it. Charlene put her arm around my shoulders and hugged.

She said, "This is good, honey. You didn't love Ronnie anyway."

I knew it was true. I'd been angry, not hurt, when I caught Ronnie with Estelle, like he went back on a business deal. Plus, one look at Ben Williamson's eyes and all over my body, bells clanged and lights flashed. Boy, howdy. And I'd thought all my fuses were blown.

No, I told myself. No men. What you need is a nice stint in a convent. But what I was seeing were those eyes.

Marci handed me my keys. "I saw the paper. *Brigadoon* opens October tenth, huh?"

I cringed and turned to Charlene. Thanks to a few unwitting comments about her ability to sew a straight seam, Kitty had appointed Charlene wardrobe mistress for the Big Comeback. Being as foolish as I was and an even bigger sap, she'd accepted.

Charlene rolled her eyes. "Don't even say it. A month away?" Her eyes met mine and held them a second. "That's Kitty's birthday, isn't it?"

"I know. It's crazy, but—"

She stopped me. "You're going to try to do it."

I pushed my lips together into a tight line and nodded.

Charlene sighed. "If we can rent the kilts for the guys, I can fudge the dresses with stuff from the Salvation Army. I'll be hemming skirts with masking tape a half hour before curtain; I just know it." Then she gave me another hug. "We'll manage."

Charlene looked down at my toes. "Speaking as your attorney, a spectacular, high-profile breakup involving a politician and a portable toilet is bad enough, but a breakup in shoes that ugly is simply unacceptable."

I eyed my knobbly-soled, duck-like feet.

"I have my Pumas in the car," I said.

Charlene grabbed my arm and led me toward her white Jeep Cherokee. "I think this situation calls for something more powerful than Pumas. You, girlfriend, are in need of a serious shoe intervention. Luckily, I'm a trained professional."

I smiled, feeling every bit of why Charlene had been my best friend as long as I'd known her and would be still, no matter how many Ronnies came and went in both our lives.

We drove the old highway east, inland from the lake, past the battered sign: *Birthplace of itty London*, the "K" having peeled off decades ago.

I told Charlene about the break-in at the Egyptian, how the backdrop had been slashed and destroyed.

"I don't know," I finished. "Maybe it was just kids. Creepy kids with knives and sex issues."

"Could be. We've got plenty of them," she said turning onto the interstate. "Everybody does."

We headed south and half an hour later exited among a forest of signs for fast-food restaurants and designer outlets.

"Even with this break-in, you want to try to open the show on Kitty's birthday?" she asked.

"The planets are aligned." I rolled my eyes. "If the Egyptian's Big Comeback fails because we miss the alignment or tri-une, or whatever-the-heck it is, I'll never hear the end of it."

Charlene was silent until we pulled into the parking lot and found a space.

"Kate?" She put the car in park and looked at me. "Maybe that would be a good thing. You know, if Kitty blamed you, or the stars, or whatever for the theatre staying closed?"

I stopped, my hand on the cool metal door handle. I tried to picture telling the woman who had turned down several bona fide chances at her own "Big Comeback" to raise me that I couldn't do my part to reopen the Egyptian—that a sleazy vandal had made it impossible for me to even try.

"Kitty deserves a chance to get the Egyptian rolling again," I said. "It isn't Hollywood, but it's all she's got left."

Charlene shook her head and grinned at me. She patted my arm. "She's got one more thing left. She's got you."

In the outlet mall, we made a beeline for Imelda's Closet, and my best friend again showed me why the University of Michigan gave her a free ride at the age of fifteen. She unearthed a pair of black kitten-heeled Jimmy Choo boots in my size for 70 percent off.

Amazing woman, Charlene.

I was newly unemployed and two out of three credit cards hovered near maximum load, but saving 70 percent on Jimmy Choo, as the good counselor pointed out, is like actually making money.

Back at the courthouse, Charlene dropped me at my car and headed into the jail to meet her newest client, LaDonna MacRae.

SIX

Fifteen minutes later, I parked in front of the Egyptian. The marquee was dark, but held the ominously hopeful statement "Opening Soon." I pushed the button to pop my trunk and pulled out my clubs. Hoisting my golf bag over my shoulder, I closed the hatch and walked under the pyramid-shaped entrance canopy. I stepped between the six-foot-tall statues of Isis and Osiris with their turquoise plaster robes and black-and-gold striped head-dresses. I'd carefully repainted them last summer. They looked thoughtful as they stood guard, one on either side of the approach—like they were contemplating the afterlife, in a kitschy sort of way.

"Some guards," I said. "Where were you guys this morning when I needed you?" I unlocked the door.

Once inside, I hauled my clubs into the lobby and leaned the bag against the wall. I felt an unfamiliar tightness tapping at the small of my back—a subtle awareness that this was no longer a safe place. I yanked out my seven-iron. It was the only club I'd practiced with,

35

and if any knife-wielding Jedi Knights came back for a return performance, by golly, I didn't want to swing and miss.

I stepped into the auditorium and walked down to the broken exit door. I tugged on the rope I'd tied earlier. It seemed loose, so I brought my bicycle in from the alley and used my cable lock to fasten the door shut.

I tried not to look at the backdrop with its slashes and vile red and black scrawls. This hurt more than Ronnie, more than being arrested. I knew I should call Ben—tell him about it, but I couldn't. Not right now. I stood a few minutes in the dim glow of the ghost light, then I rubbed my eyes and began picking up paint cans.

It's good to have a dog when you've had a lousy day, someone to comfort you, to make it better. I headed backstage, unlocked the door to the back stairway, and called Ernie, my dachshund-poodle mix. His long, low, shaggy body and wispy ears and tail always reminded me of a poorly drawn Dr. Seuss character, and I smiled in spite of myself.

"Ernie," I tried again and patted my thigh.

A flash of brown sped past me and sprinted through the wings and onto the stage.

Ernie stood, his stubby legs in a puddle of sticky paint, and panted. I got there in time to see him snatch something up in his mouth. He growled and ran backstage, leaving a trail of baby-blue paw prints. He disappeared up the stairwell.

I trudged up the stairs following the paint.

"Oh Jeeze, I need this," I muttered.

"This" was what you got when you picked the special needs dog at the shelter. They'd warned me his kibbles bag wasn't quite full.

I needed bribery.

In the kitchen, I grabbed a cocktail weenie from the fridge. Partial prints turned to dots of blue and disappeared beneath the gigantic armoire that housed my television. I leaned my golf club against the armoire and got down on my knees.

Brown eyes glared at me from under shaggy brows. Something blue hung out of his long, narrow muzzle.

"Ernie, come!" I tried in my stern, training-tape voice, the one we'd learned watching "Dr. Phyllis, Dog Psychologist."

Ernie flattened his ears sideways and attempted a growl. Thanks to whatever he had stuffed in his muzzle, it came out a garbled "Mrrrowffff."

Ernie had good days and bad, this being a "bad" day. We weren't allowed to have bad days at the same time, and this one was all mine.

I held the tiny cocktail hot dog to the floor and wiggled it. A black nose snuffled out. It moved nearer the wiener and twitched furiously. Ernie scooted, combat-style, out from under the cabinet.

He gobbled up the sausage, then swished his tail like a stringy Olympic pennant. He jumped at me with excited little yips.

I lifted him in my arms and scratched his long, scraggly ears. I knew he'd been given up as hopeless. I knew the vet wanted him on doggie Prozac for life. Still, he made progress a bit at a time. So he wasn't perfect. Who was?

I buried my face in the tuft of fur behind his ear, glad to be home. A few seconds later, I put Ernie down and got back on my knees. I reached under the armoire and pulled out a soft turquoise-blue leather glove. I didn't recognize it. I put it next to the television.

SEVEN

THE NEXT MORNING I showered away as much of the day before as I could, then I made a pot of coffee, walked and fed Ernie, and sat down at the kitchen table.

Brigadoon by Kitty's birthday—I must be nuts.

Using my one remaining credit card, I made a phone call to the lighting rental company and reserved a follow spot. Our bare-bones sound equipment would have to do. We could beg or borrow props and reuse scenery, but we'd still have to rent ten kilts. Between that and the production rights to the show, the numbers would melt right off my MasterCard.

And, if we didn't break even, at 24 percent interest—let's just say I needed to find a new job. Fast.

I'd go see Howard Douglas and try to get my old job back. After all, we had something in common. The woman I'd caught Ronnie with, Estelle, was Howard's wife.

I was contemplating which suit to wear when Kitty breezed in. She wore an oversized black sweater and tiger-striped leggings, tottery black high heels, and on her head, a tasseled fez. Husband number three—the Oldsmobile—was a Shriner.

"Well, I can tell you this, it wasn't the Naked Bandit. He mugged Verna out at the Wal-Mart yesterday around noon." Kitty put the bag she'd been carrying on my kitchen table. "A person like that, with so few inhibitions, he'd make a fabulous actor. When he mugs me, I think I'll ask him to join the Players."

"Kitty, don't you dare. The guy is a nut job." I poured coffee into a cup and slid it across the table to her. "Not to mention a criminal. I can't believe you actually want to get mugged."

"Mugged and flashed. It's the flashed part that's got my attention." She began pulling items out of the grocery bag and handing them to me. "He's gotten practically everybody at the Senior Center. You'd think being a big celebrity and everything, I'd be a hot target."

Kitty made six movies in the late fifties and early sixties after a very short stint on Broadway. She'd been famous once, and the old folks here remembered her, but it'd been forty years since *Attack of the Dung Beetles*.

"I tried to tell you, but you wouldn't listen," she said.

Kitty handed me a package of frozen cannelloni. I shoved it in the freezer.

"You put it in the wrong corner." Kitty lifted up a small bag. "Here are some of those nice muffins from Muffin Mania. And some New York sharp cheddar, the white kind—you still like that, right? I know Ernie does."

Kitty smiled, broke off a chunk of cheese, and slipped it to Ernie. He thumped his tail, a one-dog fan club.

"Godiva chocolates. You simply cannot have enough chocolate at a time like this. I got you two boxes." She handed me one shiny gold box and set the other on the table.

"Put what in the wrong corner?" I asked. I slid the box on top of the refrigerator.

"The yellow couch. I'm here to help you move it. Right now."

Kitty took yoga, and she lifted weights regularly at the Senior Center. The weights weighed three pounds.

"I shouldn't have let you leave it there. It was a romantic disaster waiting to happen." She opened the box of Godivas and popped one in her mouth. "I blame myself."

"What are you talking about?"

"Feng Shui," she said around the chocolate.

"Same to you," I said.

She swallowed. "You know perfectly well what Feng Shui is." Kitty sat down at my kitchen table and ate another Godiva.

I sighed and reached for a chocolate. "Don't tell me, you took a class."

Kitty and her best friend, Verna, had taken at least a dozen classes since I'd moved back to Mudd Lake, among them, Self-Defense over Seventy, Freeing Your Inner Child, and a most unsettling Acupuncture You Can Do at Home.

The fez tassel wiggled in indignation. "You fault me my lifelong pursuit of knowledge?"

It all became clear now. The couch, a birthday gift from Kitty, was really some stealthy Chinese talisman, claiming to bring me luck while it secretly undermined the comfortable, secondhand atmosphere of my living room.

Kitty pulled a tub of Cookies 'n' Cream Häagen-Dazs out of her bag and handed it to me. In our family, you fed a cold, but you stuffed a broken heart 'til the seams split on your jeans. I was pretty sure my heart wasn't even dented, but I planned to eat the whole tub of Häagen-Dazs anyway. I finished packing my larder with refined sugar and cholesterol and sat down.

"I kept telling you to move that couch where the armoire is. It needed to be in the southwest corner—auspicious for romance. You did the opposite and disrupted your romantic energy flow." She chopped her hand across the top of her fez, karate-style. "Blocked your chi."

I put my cheek against the cool surface of my vintage Formica table and shut my eyes. Changing the subject seemed a good idea, but *Brigadoon* scared me. I didn't know for sure who the cast was, but I'd bet there wasn't a soul in it under seventy.

Instead I said, "I saw a dead man yesterday—the murdered guy. I got deputized."

Kitty put down her third piece of chocolate and stared.

I told her about the untimely demise of the spikey-haired man behind the plaza and about LaDonna's arrest. Her voice echoed in my head, and I felt a pang of guilt.

You're gonna help me, right? Because I think I'm being framed.

"I wish I'd seen a dead body or gotten deputized," Kitty said. "A dead body upstages a naked one five ways to Sunday." She popped the third chocolate. "Shcarrie shtuff."

EIGHT

By LUNCHTIME, I WAS dressed in my best, blue, beg-for-my-job-back suit and last year's deal of the century, my navy Stuart Weitzman pumps.

My yellow couch resided in the middle of the living room where I'd dragged it under Kitty's supervision before giving up. If weight was any indication, that sucker must've been stuffed with some mighty heavy chi.

I set out for the corner and Mama's Deli, Howard Douglas's favorite place to lunch. A few leaves swirled around my ankles, the first casualties of fall. The Acadia Building's eight-foot granite Indians and subdued art deco fixtures stood in solemn contrast to the colorful plaster and riotous Egyptian baroque of the theatre.

I passed the Acadia's windows, and neon signs for Fast Eddie's Pawn Shop, Lickity-Split Paycheck Advances, and Benny's Bail Bonds glowed in the overcast gloom of the day. Our town's seedy underbelly enjoyed one-stop shopping at the Acadia.

Even Charlene's practice was here. I glanced up at the rectangle of brightness on the second floor—her office. I loved having her next door, but like the Egyptian Theatre, this building deserved better.

I held my breath as I swung through Mama's screen door, not just because I was nervous about asking for my old job back, but because everyone held their breath when they walked in here. The initial blast from Mama's homemade sauerkraut could put a person off her feed for a whole day.

Chatter bounced off the pressed tin ceiling and ricocheted from the white pine hardwood floors. I spotted Howard Douglas's thick mane of silvery-white hair.

I made my legs work and walked to where he sat, his usual booth next to the back room. Locals called that room the Sometimes Bar because Charlene's mother, the mom in Mama's, opened it Wednesday through Saturday after five—if she felt like it.

"Hi, Howard."

"Oh, it's you." He folded his copy of the *Mudd Lake Eavesdropper* and slid it away.

"Mind if I sit down?"

He raised his palm in a gesture of "whatever." I carefully scooted my only good pair of pantyhose past the duct tape repair as I slid into the red vinyl booth.

He gestured for the waitress, and she brought me an empty cup.

Pouring some coffee from the thermal carafe, I said, "I guess you heard what happened."

He nodded and tapped an article below the fold on the front page. "Mayor Assaulted in Port-o-potty Incident." My cheeks began to feel warm with embarrassment. At least the murder at the strip mall had nudged me out of top billing.

"I really screwed up," I said. "I thought Ronnie was perfect for me. I tried so hard to be logical about things."

"You can't decide love with logic. You must trust this," Howard pointed to the center of his chest, "and this." He pointed to his gut.

I was tempted to reach over and point a little lower on Howard and say, "Then how come you trusted this?"

I really needed my old job back so I bit my lip.

He looked away. His voice came out lower, just above a whisper. "I didn't fare much better. It is not the first time for Estelle, or the second . . . or the third. I filed for divorce yesterday. Besides, I believe she may be a golddigger."

Golddigger? That woman used a backhoe. She'd been married to Howard less than three years and had acquired a seven-carat diamond ring, a $120,000 Mercedes, two vacation homes, and more furs than the Imperial Russian Ballet. From a prior marriage, she even owned this building and an interior design firm that, as far as I knew, had zero clients whatsoever.

"I'm sorry, Howard." I patted his hand. I took a deep breath. "Howard, I was wondering—"

I heard a familiar voice. "Kate."

I looked up and squarely into the face of Ronnie Balfours. He sneered as he stood over our table. His blond hair was straight back and perfect, and he wore a white golf shirt and crisp khakis. The only odd thing was that he resembled a large aquamarine tabby cat. His skin was streaked all over with faded blue dye. Who knew that blue stuff was permanent?

"Got a present for you, bitch."

He shoved a large manila envelope under my nose.

"There's another one just like it tacked to the door of the Egyptian." His voice was ugly, self-satisfied. "Right where we'll aim the wrecking ball."

Wrecking ball?

The smell of sauerkraut overwhelmed me. It took all of my willpower not to toss my coffee in Ronnie's vindictive, bluish face.

"And you," he jabbed a streaky finger in Howard's direction. "Estelle's gonna take you for everything you've got—doesn't matter if she screwed the friggin' King of Siam. She's got a shark of an attorney. Putting up with your sorry ass for the last three years, I think that entitles her to half of Douglas Real Estate, don't you? I mean what's left of it, after I get through with you at Lansdowne."

Howard was deadly calm. He stood up. He was a full three inches taller than Ronnie.

"Whatever personal issues you and I have," he said, "Lansdowne is still your responsibility. Handle it."

"You can't tell me what to do." Ronnie jutted his chin out and stepped into Howard. "Don't think for a minute I'll be left holding the bag out there."

Howard's voice was very quiet, but had a razor-like edge to it. "You will handle the Lansdowne problem, or you'll be sorry—extremely, excruciatingly sorry. As for Estelle, you two deserve each other. And Ronnie, my friend, you deserve so much more. I truly hope you get it."

A chill wave lapped over me. I tossed a bill onto the table and, brushing past them both, stumbled out to the street.

I ran past the Acadia and up to the gold double doors to the theatre. I read the notice tacked there: *Condemned.*

I slid the papers out of the envelope and skimmed through a list of building violations. Words like "neighborhood blight" popped out at me. Words like "for the common good." There were almost sixty violations, from the holes in the roof to a spider infestation.

Yes, the roof had holes. Yes, we had a lot of work to do to get the place open. But this gave us two weeks to get out, and then the city was going to level the building. The building. Kitty's theatre. My home. The Big Comeback. This would kill Kitty.

Damn you, Ronnie!

The notice on the door said, "Do Not Remove Under Penalty of Law." I ripped it down. Then I seethed and bubbled the six blocks across town for my very first anger management session.

NINE

I STOMPED UP THE steps and took a seat among the fifteen or so adults that occupied the creaky bleachers of the junior high gym. I tried to unclench my teeth—to forget that Ronnie existed.

I focused on the room. My nostrils flared with every breath, and I was all too aware that Ronnie existed. I gave in to grinding my molars together as I looked around.

Everybody snuck sidelong glances at each other. A couple of folks wore biker jackets, one lady had a mail carrier's uniform. I was the only person in a business suit except for a tiny, sixty-ish lady with gray hair coiled into a tight doorknob atop her head.

The sixty-ish lady stepped out onto the wood floor in front of us. She was about to speak when the double doors to the gym burst open, and a young woman with fluorescent turquoise hair rushed in.

"Sorry I'm late," she called. She brushed past the older woman and headed for the bleachers.

The doorknob-headed woman pointed her finger at the girl. "Stop . . . right . . . there, Patrice." The tiny woman jerked her finger for emphasis at each word. "YOU'RE LATE! You know better than to be late for this class. If you are late ever again, you WILL GO TO JAIL." The tiny woman was yelling now. Her doorknob-like bun unraveled slightly. A gray coil bobbed up and down beside her head, punctuating each word.

"I'm sorry, Doctor Al," the young woman said.

I noticed a silvery glint in the girl's mouth. It looked like a live minnow—no, a tongue stud.

"How many TIMES DO YOU HAVE TO COME HERE TO GET IT RIGHT?" The woman was screaming now. "ARE YOU AN IDIOT?"

The bleachers gave out a series of tortured squeaking sounds as everyone shifted uncomfortably.

"Um . . . It won't happen again. I'm sorry." The girl seemed small, intimidated, even though she was about a foot taller than the woman.

Doctor Al stared up at the girl for a minute. Then she looked up at the bleachers as if she'd just noticed us.

"I'm Doctor Al, and I seem to have hyperventilated. I need to take five minutes to recompose."

I held my breath and waited to see if this was some kind of joke—some kind of "what not to do" demonstration. Doctor Al grabbed her big black purse from the bleachers and walked out the double doors to the hallway.

The blue-headed girl seemed to recognize me. She bounded up the stairs and took the seat next to me on the bench.

"Hi, I'm Patrice," she said.

I nodded to her and flashed the twitchy muscle spasm that these days passed for my smile.

A few minutes later, Doctor Al returned to the gym. Her hair was tucked back into its fist-like little knob. She set her purse on the bleacher next to a large box. The big bag clinked when it hit the wood.

Dr. Al started over. "I'm Dr. Alice Parker. My patients call me Dr. Al. Anger got you all into trouble with the law, so you are now my patients, like it or not. Welcome to Anger Management 101."

Everybody snuck more looks at each other.

"Does anyone here know what kind of emotion anger is?" Dr. Al asked.

A guy built like a refrigerator and wearing a leather jacket with "Devil's Cheerleaders" emblazoned across the shoulder blades raised his hand. "I believe it's referred to as a secondary emotion."

Who's he? Hell's psych professor?

"That's right. Anger is a secondary emotion. That means you feel something else first; offended, cornered, beaten down, frustrated."

Or all of them at once. I fidgeted on the rickety wooden bench. I felt my nostrils stretch wide again as my breathing sped up.

"When you are angry, count to ten. That's first."

I whispered through gritted teeth, "Ronnie, you bastard, one. Ronnie, you bastard, two—"

"Our following sessions will be about the appropriate ways to communicate our true feelings. Today though, we'll have a bit of an exercise. Blowing off a little steam helps you get to your true emotions." She lowered her penciled-in eyebrows, leaned her head down, and looked up at us from beady, red-rimmed eyes. She looked like a small, ticked-off rodent. "You are only to blow off steam at inanimate objects. Understand?"

When I got through with Ronnie, he'd *be* an inanimate object.

Dr. Al's glance traveled over the crowd. "I need two volunteers to start us off."

I shrank down low on the bench, hunched my shoulders, and tried not to snort.

My blue-headed neighbor raised an arm in the air and wiggled her fingers. "I'm sorry I was late, Doctor Al. Let me make it up." She pointed at herself from on high. "I'll volunteer."

"You were late?" Dr. Al asked.

Patrice put her arm down and frowned. I glanced at the psych guy. His eyes went wide.

Dr. Al looked at Patrice, then at me. "Perfect. Yes, come down here you—and you." She poked toward me with a knobby finger.

Crud.

Patrice bounced her way down the steps. I hunched lower. I thought of bolting for the door. Then I thought of jail. I climbed down and stood next to Patrice with her tattered hip-huggers, open-toed Birkenstocks, and "Bloodweasels World Annihilation Tour" t-shirt.

When we faced Dr. Al, I smelled booze.

A row of industrial-looking canvas punching bags hung on chains from the thirty-foot ceiling. We stood next to a crate of oversized plastic bats. She picked up a big yellow bat for Patrice and handed me a bright red one.

I looked down at the bat. I didn't trust myself to have a weapon in my hand, albeit a clown-like plastic one.

"I need your names, please."

Patrice called out, "Patrice Stikowski." She waved at the crowd. "And yours?" she asked.

I focused my eyes on my shoes. "Kate London," I said in a low voice.

"I knew it," Patrice said. "Am I good or what?"

A few people gasped. A tough-looking woman with alarmingly big muscles and very short hair leaned over to her neighbor and whispered loudly, "She's the one knocked Balfours down the hill in the crapper." Then a windstorm of whispering broke out all through the group.

I moved my gaze from my tapered navy toes to the bat. I squinted at it and squeezed until my knuckles went white.

Dr. Al didn't seem to hear the crowd. "I want you to take all your anger and aim it at the punching bags," she said. She slapped one of the canvas bags with her hand and waited.

Patrice didn't hesitate a nano-second.

Whap. The bat connected hard, and her canvas bag bounced a little on its chain.

"Cool," she said. "I love this part."

I tapped my bat on the wooden floor a few times while adrenaline fizzed through my bloodstream.

Dr. Al said, "Kate, you may begin."

Okay, it's jail time or this. I can do this. I can calmly do this.

I brushed at the bag with my bat.

Someone in the crowd yelled, "Pretend it's Ronnie."

Another called out, "I didn't vote for the jerk. Hit him once for me."

I took a swing.

Dr. Al said, "You can do better than that. Smack it like you mean it."

I took a hefty poke. My fellow detainees cheered.

I did it again. *Fwoomp!!*

It felt pretty good. A couple of bags down from me, Patrice was whacking away.

She threw her head back and yelled, "Wahoo!" She pounded her bag in the side.

Dr. Al brought the rest of the class onto the floor, and they began fwomping and whapping at their respective bags.

I pictured Ronnie's face as he proposed. "Liar," I muttered. *Whomp.* I batted the bag at face level.

I thought about him filing assault charges against me. *Whaap!*

I smacked the thing again with gusto. I started really getting into it.

Fwaap. I hit the bag at gut level.

I got to the big one. "You pig. You stay away from our theatre!"

I aimed low on the bag and jabbed him in his imaginary crotch, then I smacked it a few times around shoulder level. I finished off by bashing the bag about twenty times in a row around where Ronnie's skull would be.

I threw my head back and screamed, "Die, Ronnie, die! I hate you! You'll never get the Egyptian!"

Boy, that felt good.

I noticed when I finished that the rest of the group had stopped beating their punching bags. Everyone was watching me.

Patrice called over, "Awesome! Just awesome!"

"Everyone, that was excellent," Dr. Al said. "You may go."

I turned to head for the door.

Dr. Al was making notes on a clipboard. "Not you," she jabbed that knobby finger in my direction. "You, stay here."

TEN

My classmates filed out of the gym. Some of them glanced over their shoulders at me as they pushed through the double doors. I felt my cheeks get hot, and sweat started to bloom under my arms and on my forehead.

Patrice, the last to leave, hesitated.

"YOU." Dr. Al's voice was snappish. She wiggled her finger at the door. "GO."

"I'll wait for you outside," Patrice said and scooted out the door.

And Dr. Al and I were alone. I hovered next to her while she made furious notes on her clipboard.

Without looking up she said, "I'm recommending a remedial class for you, one-on-one, intensive work, starting at nine tomorrow, every day for a week."

"Wait a minute, I did what you told me to do. I did exactly what you told me to do." My anger was exhausted, which was probably good since I was still choking my bat.

"You did it a little too well." She made more notes on her clipboard. She lowered her eyebrows and looked at me, then she reached for my bat and tossed it in a cardboard box with the others.

"Can we talk about this? Please?" I said.

"No."

"Just let me come back with the group next week. My plate's pretty full now and . . ."

Dr. Al stood over the bat box while I was talking. It looked like she was taking inventory. The box was almost as big as she was. She placed her clipboard on the bleacher, strained over the edge, and came up with a flaming orange bat. She held the bat over her head with both hands and brought it down, whacking the lowest bleacher. Hard. Really hard. So hard, the sound reverberated through the empty gymnasium. The end of her clipboard lifted up in the air and slapped down, and her purse flew off the bench and onto the wood floor. Something broke and an amber liquid that smelled like whiskey leaked out. Dr. Al stared at it.

She whipped around. She screeched, "What part of NO do you NOT UNDERSTAND??"

I realized my jaw was hanging open and snapped it shut.

Through clenched teeth she said, "You are making me angry. Anger is BAD. YOU SHOULD KNOW! YOU HAVE NO CONTROL OVER YOURS! You WILL be here tomorrow at nine A.M. for remedial anger management. OR ELSE."

I managed a nod, snatched up my purse and papers, and scooted out the door.

* * *

Patrice was waiting for me in the lot. "That was weird, huh?"

"I'd say so."

"It always is," she said. "I'm LaDonna's friend, Deputy Kate. Sheriff Ben told me where to find you. He said we were in the same class." She grinned at me. "You look just like your grandma in her old movies. That's how I knew it was you."

I was dumbfounded.

"Look, I'm not—"

"So I just wanted to say, you know, LaDonna's like, really grateful. She told Sheriff Ben how you guys talked in the car, how she felt better knowing he had a deputy to help. Sheriff Ben said what a big help you are. He said when I saw you, I should give you this envelope."

I took the manila envelope and peeked inside. It contained a tin star. Keeping it in the envelope, I made out the etched outline of the droopy-jowled cartoon character "Deputy Dawg." This was the badge I'd had as a kid. Somewhere along the line, I must've given it to him.

Very funny.

Patrice leaned toward the envelope. I snapped it shut.

"Is it important?"

"Not really," I said. "If you see Sheriff Ben, be sure to thank him."

As soon as I got out of here, I planned to buy one of those bats and go after Ronnie first, then I'd "thank" Ben myself.

"LaDonna and I thought of something," Patrice said. "We told Sheriff Ben. We thought we should tell you, too. We think Taz, you know, like the dead guy? He joined a religious cult or something, cuz when he saw LaDonna at BatCave, he wanted her to keep his monk's robe."

A monk's robe?

I stared at her. "Did LaDonna describe this robe to you?"

"I saw it myself out at BatCave that morning. It was brown burlap with a pointy hood, kind of cheesy looking."

I caught my breath.

Obi-Wan Kenobi. Taz was our vandal.

"Patrice, this is great information." I patted her shoulder. "Thanks for telling me about it."

Patrice slipped on a pair of thin leather gloves, unlocked a metallic green moped from a clamp around a no parking sign, and kicked back the kickstand. She hopped on and started the engine.

"No problem, Deputy Kate. See ya."

I called after her. "Wait, I'm not—"

Her engine revved, drowning me out.

ELEVEN

I walked back to Main Street and headed straight to Charlene's. In her lobby, I waved to Marci. Without removing the phone receiver from her ear, she wiggled her fingers and motioned me past.

Charlene sat behind her shabby-but-not-so-chic secondhand desk. It was the size of a football field, and she used every inch. She was sandwiched between stacks of manila files that stood a foot high to her left and right. Another file lay open in front of her.

Tuesdays were court days so she wore a St. John suit, camel with navy trim. The suit must be for LaDonna. Charlene only dressed up to go to court, and then only if the client looked at serious jail time.

A stray wisp of her brown hair had escaped her chignon, and she tucked it back in without looking up. Then she raised her head and grinned at me.

"I saw Ronnie this morning; he looks like a lava lamp." She returned her attention to the open file and muttered, "Let me just finish here. This county really needs another public defender."

I plopped into the worn leather chair opposite her desk and waited.

When she closed the file, I held the condemnation notice under my chin, then I handed her the papers.

Her eyes grew large. "Oh my God. That jerk."

She picked up the top sheet and scanned through the rest of the documents. She frowned and put the papers down.

"I can't believe this. I really can't," I said. I grabbed a tissue and started twisting it around itself, wringing an imaginary, blue-streaked neck.

"Yeah. This is nasty. What they plan to do is flatten the Egyptian and take the land underneath as payment for the demolition."

"And get this," I said, "the guy that was murdered out at Medication Nation Plaza, I think he's the one that vandalized the Egyptian yesterday. Trashed the stage and the backdrop."

I told her about the vandal's theft of the Obi-Wan Kenobi robe, and my conversation with Patrice.

"Yeah, I heard about that robe. So that was the Obi-Wan costume? Weird. There's an outside chance that could help LaDonna. I don't see how it helps you with this, though." She lifted the condemnation notice and dropped it.

I blew my nose on the imaginary Ronnie. "Me neither."

Charlene scanned the papers. "According to this letter, the town council talked about condemning the Egyptian six months ago. Looks like Ronnie vetoed it."

"Six months ago? And he never told me?"

"Maybe he was trying to protect you."

"Some protection." I shook my head. I tried to wrap my mind around this. "They can't just go around flattening people's buildings, can they?"

"The problem is, the city sent you a letter over a year ago, a list of things to fix, and you didn't respond. That's why they can give you so little time before they fire up the bulldozer."

"Hey!"

"Sorry . . . But technically you're in violation of a bunch of dangerous building codes," she said. "If you weren't living there, they could have done it already. They're well within their legal rights."

"They didn't send me any letter!"

She rifled through the packet and handed it to me. It was certified, addressed to Kitty. Kitty, whose bills were all sent to me because she threw out anything that wasn't *Playbill*, fan mail, or checks from the Screen Actors Guild pension plan. And Ronnie knew it.

Charlene and I stared at each other.

"That bastard. This'll break Kitty's heart."

Charlene sighed. "God . . . I know."

"There's got to be something I can do," I said. I ran my hands through my hair. "Some way to stop this."

I got up and walked to the window. The wind had kicked up, forming whitecaps on the lake. In the distance, an ore freighter moved slowly through the choppy waters.

Charlene swiveled in her chair. "Kitty managed for the two years after she closed the theatre. She'll be okay."

Kitty'd managed by staying home in her nightclothes for most of those two years. It had been excruciating to watch. After a couple of visits home, seeing her like that, I realized she wasn't snapping out of it, and I moved back.

"You've seen the change in her since we started renovations," I said. I sat back down. "I can't let Ronnie take that away." I strangled another Kleenex. "I won't."

"Town council meets next Monday at seven," Charlene said. "We'll get you on their agenda, and you can try to get them to reverse this, explain about the letter, about your plans. I don't think they'll be too keen on it, but that's about all I can think of to do."

"Oh God." I put my face in my hands. "A town council meeting with Ronnie in charge. I am so screwed."

She frowned. "I know."

* * *

My answering machine was blinking when I got home.

Two messages from Ronnie: "Kate, I need to talk to you." The first was time-stamped around one. The second, a bit later when I'd been at Charlene's: "Kate, call me right away. We need to talk."

I thumbed my nose at the phone. I'd have to face him next Monday, but I didn't have to do it today.

I nuked some frozen cannelloni, fed and walked Ernie, and wearing my pajama bottoms, a t-shirt, and new boots, opened a bottle of Merlot. After I drank most of it, curiosity or lack of judgment got the better of me, and I dialed Ronnie's number. I stuck my toes out in front of me and turned my ankles first one way and then the other. My life sucked big red baboon bottoms, but my Jimmy Choos were gorgeous.

The phone continued to ring.

Ronnie's voicemail finally went off. Relieved, I hung up, slipped off my boots, and fell into bed.

TWELVE

EARLY THE NEXT MORNING, I awoke to Ernie scratching at the outside door.

"Go back to sleep," I mumbled into my pillow.

He scratched some more and whimpered. I flipped over on my back and sat bolt upright. One thought did it—a thought that strikes fear in the hearts of dog owners everywhere—diarrhea.

"Hold on, hold on," I said.

I jumped out of bed and stuck my head into the hall. Ernie stood at the door and panted at me, his tail stiff in the air.

I pulled a hooded sweatshirt over my Chris Isaak t-shirt. I didn't waste time changing out of my pajama bottoms or combing my tangled curls. I slipped my bare feet into my Pumas.

We headed for the meager grassy strip in front of the theatre. Ernie scrambled toward my car and yipped. He scooted to the full extension of his retractable leash and pulled hard on his black nylon harness. His furry paws swam frantically in the grass while I reeled him back like a marlin. I held the leash taut as he sniffed the air in the direction of my rear bumper. He barked at my trunk and growled hard enough to cause his ears to vibrate.

"Hey you! Settle down . . . now!"

Just what I needed to go with my messed up life: a hallucinating dachshund-mix. I bent down and patted him. This caused him to jump about a foot, the equivalent of me jumping over the Egyptian Theatre, then he threw his head back and howled. Dogs his size don't howl well. It came out more like the cock-a-doodle-doo of a forlorn rooster.

"Oh for pity's sake. There is nothing in that trunk but air."

Ernie crowed mournfully and stared first at me, then at the bumper.

"Oh, all right!"

I had my keys in my pocket so I pulled them out and aimed the remote clicker at the back of the car. The trunk creaked out a plea for WD-40 as it opened.

"See, I told you . . ."

At first I thought someone had put old clothes in my car. I stepped closer and recognized a familiar leather jacket, then the whole world seemed to cartwheel out of control. I saw a hand—a very pale hand, faintly stained aquamarine. Something dark red and sticky looking was matted in the fringe of blonde hair above the collar.

My own head seemed to be floating about six feet above my shoulders while my body felt as heavy and unmoving as a concrete garden gnome. I swallowed back the sour taste of bile that rose up in my throat. Ronnie Balfours was dead. In my trunk. Deader than a greenish-blue doornail.

THIRTEEN

ERNIE BOUNCED HIS FRONT legs against the bumper. I tugged his leash back and slid the sleeve of my sweater over my fingers. Touching as little of the trunk as possible, I eased the lid down and latched it, all the while making a silent "eek" grimace.

"Sorry," I said to Ronnie's corpse.

I ran with Ernie through the narrow alley and up the stairs. Once inside, I went into the kitchen and let the door swing closed. I reached into the cookie jar, grabbed some diversionary dog biscuits, and tossed them to the floor.

It made me very nervous to be unable to see my car. I grabbed my cell phone and pressed 9-1-1 as I headed back outside.

I pulled open the front door and was just about to hit send when I stepped directly into an extremely solid, tan-uniformed chest.

"Umfh," I muttered into it.

The chest belonged to Ben Williamson.

I stumbled back a few feet. In one hand, he held a clipboard, in the other, a bag from Muffin Mania. He took a step forward.

I caught my breath and started, "Ben . . ."

He grinned. "Deputy Kate—"

"Ben, not now, I'm . . . he's—"

"Kate, you can't remove that condemnation notice." He held up the clipboard. "I'm going to put a fresh one up this time, but touch it again, and I'll give you a ticket."

At that moment, Ernie scooted out of the swinging kitchen door and, stringy ears flying backwards, galloped toward Ben.

"Be careful. He bites strangers!" I grabbed for Ernie's harness and missed.

Ernie swished his tail and snuffled Ben's shoe. Ben shifted the bag to the hand with the clipboard and reached down. He scratched Ernie's ear.

"Hey, buddy."

Ernie, his memory as blank as a freshly shaken Etch-a-Sketch, flopped over on his back to have his long tummy rubbed. I, on the other hand, saw little clear dots again.

Ben glanced up at me. He wiggled the muffin bag and the clipboard. "The condemnation notice. And a muffin, if you want it."

The room seemed to be spinning. "What?"

"The condemnation notice—you can't remove it." His brow furrowed. "Kate? . . . Are you listening to me?"

I gripped the doorknob and used it to support my wobbly legs. I tried to keep my teeth from chattering.

"It's Ronnie . . . he's um . . . Ben, you need to come with me."

I reached for the stair railing. Ben followed me onto the landing, eased Ernie's snuffling nose back inside, and shut the door.

My head still felt like a leaky helium balloon, and my legs shook as I began to climb back down the stairs. Ben followed in confused silence.

We got a few feet away from my car. "He's in there," I said.

I swallowed. My mouth felt like it was full of sand. I hit the button on my key ring, and the hatch squeaked its way back up. Ben took a few more steps and peered into the trunk. That's when the poor guy dropped his muffins.

He recovered himself quickly and stooped to pick up the white paper bag. As he bent, his eyes stayed glued to mine. He stood, tossed the muffin bag and clipboard on the lawn, and felt Ronnie's neck for a pulse. We both knew it was a hollow gesture.

"His color looks awful," Ben said. "Kinda greenish-blue." He looked up. "Oh . . ."

After a few seconds, he moved his attention to the head wound. His glance kept bouncing from Ronnie to me. I didn't move.

"What happened?"

"I don't know. I mean, I just, I found him in there . . . like that, a few minutes ago." I swallowed the bitter taste and fought to keep my voice steady.

"You just found him here? In the trunk of your car?" He took a step toward me. "Dead?" he added somewhat unnecessarily.

He took another step and put his right hand on his holster.

"You don't think I would actually . . . ? Ben, c'mon."

Thoughts ping-ponged in my head. I could bolt down the alley. Ben wouldn't shoot me, not really, would he? My eyes slid toward the passage between the buildings.

"Let's just stay calm." He took another step toward me, moved his hand from the gun, and unhooked his handcuffs from his belt.

"I'm not going to jump to any conclusions here." He put his left hand on my shoulder.

To a passerby who couldn't see the trunk, the hand on my shoulder would have looked like a polite gesture—friendly even, but the weight of it felt heavy, just short of physical restraint.

"Don't panic on me, Katie."

Charlene appeared at the doorway to the Acadia Building. Her jogging suit glowed like a lime-green beacon of hope in a sea of disaster. She held a large to-go cup from Mama's, and her over-stuffed laptop bag was slung over her shoulder.

"Hey, you all right?" she called.

"No!" I hollered.

She trotted toward us.

"Ronnie's dead. He's in the trunk of my car." My voice climbed upward and threatened to crack into tearful pieces.

Charlene stepped over to the trunk. She swallowed a sharp intake of breath and backed away. By the time she turned toward us, her face was unreadable. She extended her finger around the Styrofoam coffee cup and aimed it at me.

"Not another word."

Charlene showed Ben the trunk button on the armrest. She told him she would vouch for the fact that I never, ever locked my car.

"Anybody could have dumped Ronnie in there as easily as dumping him on a park bench," she said.

Ben agreed that was a great theory. He said he sincerely hoped it was true. Then he cuffed me, read me my rights, and put me in the back of his SUV.

As we once again made our way to the jail, I leaned my head against the cool glass of the window. I thought about Ronnie and felt a tightening in my chest and throat. He wasn't the person I'd thought he was, not by a long shot, but that didn't mean he deserved to have his skull whacked in.

Looking back, his messages last night had sounded odd, a little frightened. I wished that I'd tried his cell instead of his home number. I might have reached him.

Ben's eyes met mine in the rearview. They were as clear and dark blue as the lake.

"Kate, what happened?"

"Charlene doesn't want me talking about it," I said.

"Okay. I don't blame her. I mean it sure as heck looks like you . . ." he stopped himself and smacked his hand against the steering wheel.

I started to speak but stopped myself, too.

"Okay . . . okay. We won't talk about it," he said. He looked away, focusing on the road. "I hate my job," he muttered. "I truly hate it."

"I hate your job, too," I said. "Especially the part where you arrest me."

FOURTEEN

BEN HANDED ME OFF to a female guard. When she read the papers he'd given her, her lower jaw unhinged showing a pink wad of gum nestled next to her molar. She stared at me, then snapped her jaw closed so hard I heard her teeth clack.

She took a few seconds to recover. In a smarmy voice she said, "Well, well, well. If this keeps up, Elk County'll have to quit borrowing our jail and build its own—with an expanded ladies' wing."

She snickered and flashed me the pink wad again; then she made me take off my sweatshirt and pull the laces out of my sneakers.

I gulped. They hadn't done any of this the other day.

We walked down the hall. Someone snored in the drunk-tank. I was glad he didn't wake up; I was very aware of being braless and in pajama bottoms.

The one and only time I saw this jail was on a tour with my Brownie troop when I was seven, and it hadn't changed. Males still got private rooms, females all got tossed together in one big cell, like a poorly planned aquarium. We were headed to the end of the hall, straight for LaDonna.

LaDonna held the bars with both hands and pressed her face between them. Her makeup was gone and without it she looked to be about thirteen. She wore an orange Oscenada County jumpsuit.

"Hey," LaDonna said. She sent me a small smile and wiggled her fingers at me through the bars. I noticed with amazement that she had ten, tiny, perfect white skulls on her black fingernails.

"Hi." I wiggled my fingers back from under the cuffs.

The guard unlocked my hands. "Wave at her all you want, now." She shoved me into the cell.

The guard clanked the door across the bars and slammed it shut. Limping on her walking cast, LaDonna took a step toward me.

I sighed and plunked myself down on one of the grimy striped mattress pads. The wire mesh of the bunk bit through it into my thighs. I tipped my head back and looked up at the institutional green ceiling. Heavy wire grid covered the high slash-like windows, and boxy cages surrounded the harsh fluorescent ceiling lights. Even the fixtures here were incarcerated.

"Are you undercover again?" LaDonna stood over me and eyed my baggy cherry-print pajama bottoms.

A thought niggled and chewed at the edges of my brain. Taz trashed the Egyptian's stage and less than two hours later he was dead. Ronnie condemned the Egyptian. The next morning, he was dead. I looked down at my legs and back at LaDonna. I nodded.

"Yeah, undercover."

"So, what are you doing in here? I thought you were supposed to help. You want me to confess or something?" She met my eyes and held them. "'Cuz I didn't do it."

I was silent a long moment while our eyes remained locked. "I'm thinking I believe that," I said. "Tell me what happened the other day."

She eased her way down on the bunk next to me. She extended her cast and watched me another minute.

"I'll try to help," I said. "Just tell me what you know."

She kept her head down and picked at the skull on her left thumb, exposing more of the black polish underneath.

"Taz was my old boyfriend, treated me real bad. He came to BatCave Music that morning, where I worked—said he scored some coin. He wanted me to run away with him." She lifted her foot and looked at the cast. "He did this with a tire iron a month or so ago."

My mouth went dry.

"Yeah, right, like I'm gonna go anywhere with that dude," she said. She wiggled her cast. "I told him to go wee-wee up a rope."

I nodded. "Good for you."

The ol' wee-wee up a rope. I knew it well.

"So he like, shoved that weird robe at me and did like, his nice-guy number? When it didn't work, he knocked over a CD rack, punched a hole in the wall, and left." She rubbed the last remnant of skull from her thumb.

"You said he came into money. Do you know where he got it?"

"A job or something? Maybe dope. Who knows?" She moved on to her index finger. Flecks of white landed on her jumpsuit. "Anyway, I went outside at my usual time. For a smoke? And there's Taz with that big, old knife planted in his back like a frickin' American flag. I freaked. I must've touched him because they found a smear of blood on my hand."

She wiped imaginary blood on her jumpsuit and resumed picking at her finger. I did a quick flashback to that day, to her bloody hand, and my pulse quickened. That had looked like a lot more blood than a smear.

She looked up. "Man-oh-man, it was gross. And did you see my *car*?"

"Yeah." I nodded, as dots connected in my cranium. The spray paint on that car—I had the same color spewed all over my slashed Scottish highlands.

"Some old lady from Medication Nation came out back and saw me with Taz. When she screamed, I bolted."

I told her what I knew about the robe—how Taz had vandalized the Egyptian. I asked if she'd heard him mention Ronnie or the theatre. She hadn't.

"Who do you think killed him?" I asked. "Any ideas?"

"He was begging for it from about ten different directions." She brushed off her jumpsuit. "He hung out with a lot of nasty dudes. He was real bad. Evil."

I didn't doubt it for a second. The guy's hair had even looked dangerous to me; scary and threatening, and it was deceased hair at the time.

I sat in silence, LaDonna next to me. My thoughts zinged and careened from one scenario to another. Who could've killed Ronnie? Was it really tied to Taz or just coincidence?

I'd never seen Howard as mad as I had at Mama's. Sure, Ronnie'd been taking unauthorized nature tours with Howard's wife—

of Howard's wife, but that confrontation—it was all about Lansdowne.

What was going on out there?

I heard footsteps and turned to see Ben Williamson walking toward us.

"Hey, LaDonna, how're you doing?"

"I'm all right, Sheriff Ben," LaDonna said.

Ben raked the door open. "You need anything? Floss? A toothbrush maybe? I've got lots of spares here."

"Nah, I'm set. I just told your deputy here some stuff about Taz. I hope it helps."

Ben shot me a glance. "C'mon, let's go," he said, ". . . deputy." He grabbed my arm, and we started down the hall.

"That was very funny—sending me that badge," I said.

He kept his voice low. "You asked for it. You were the one who told LaDonna you were a deputy," he said. "Pretended like you could help her."

"You started the deputy thing, and besides I never told her I could help." I avoided his eyes. "Not until just now, anyway."

I peeked over at him. He glared at me.

"Oh. Great," he said. "Just great."

I had no clue how to help LaDonna. None at all. I felt another twinge of guilt. As we kept walking, it was nudged out by fear for my own skin.

He cleared his throat. "Sorry about the star. It was just . . . a joke."

The anger and frustration I felt toward Ben had more to do with the past than the present. Nevertheless, I glared at him and folded my arms across my ribcage.

My voice came out shrill. "Come to think of it, why didn't I just arrest myself this morning? I mean, I had the star—I could've saved you the trouble."

He kept his eyes straight ahead. "Technically, this isn't an arrest. This is questioning."

"Hah!" I said. "Jail in my pajamas. I call it arrest." I gestured to my outfit.

His glance bounced down to my Chris Isaak t-shirt, then back up again. Ben's eyes had the ability to change color from blue to gray like optical mood rings. Right now they were steel gray.

Ben looked down again at my t-shirt and pajama bottoms. "If you're gonna be a deputy, we've got to get you better uniforms," he said.

"Ha, ha." I glared at him again.

Ben's gaze returned to my chest. "Didn't I buy you that t-shirt?"

I looked down at my braless body. Blood rose into my face until my hair follicles tingled. Simultaneously, I realized three things: one—my favorite shirt came from a man who dumped me over fifteen years ago, two—my breasts definitely looked better with a bra, and three—when things are bad, they can always get worse.

* * *

Ben led me to a small room with a scarred metal table surrounded by several rickety orange plastic chairs. He let go of my arm and pulled one out.

"Sit down."

The chair rocked a little on its uneven legs, and I jerked as if I were about to fall over.

Charlene stepped through the door. As soon as I saw her, all the oxygen left the room at once, and I started gasping, sucking in little Lamaze-like breaths while perspiration trickled down my armpits.

Gone was her lime-green jogging suit. She'd replaced it with a black and white Chanel cut in knife-sharp tailored lines and a crisp white blouse. She'd twisted and pinned her ponytail into a tight, unforgiving bun at the back of her head, and she wore her very best black Via Spiga heels.

"I'll give you guys ten minutes," Ben said, "then we'll try to get to the bottom of this."

He closed the door. I heard a lock click.

FIFTEEN

CHARLENE SAT DOWN ACROSS from me and put her hands over mine on the cold table.

"How're you holding up?" she asked. Her deep brown eyes locked on mine and wouldn't let go.

I swallowed. "I was better until I saw you. You look so . . . You . . . I mean . . . You wore your *Via Spigas!*" I wailed.

Charlene nodded slowly and patted my hand.

"Well, yes. A dead fiancé stuffed in your trunk—that pretty much requires my Via Spiga-level defense strategy." Her eyes continued to drill through me, one layer at a time. "You're going to be okay, Kate. You're one of the strongest people I know, but you don't like to trust people. I need you to trust me."

Those eyes never wavered, never blinked. My own eyes welled up, and I managed to nod my head yes. I slid the trash can over in case the shark circling in my stomach decided to escape. Charlene gave my hand a final pat.

"Just follow my lead. Do not offer any information unless I tell you to." Charlene opened her briefcase and pulled out a legal pad. She slapped it on the table. "Okay?"

I nodded, swallowed hard, and gripped the edge of the table with both hands.

Charlene straightened and tucked an errant wisp of hair back into her bun.

"Showtime," she said.

"You know I have stage fright." I tried a wobbly grin. It fell off at the corners, and I squeezed my eyes shut.

Charlene walked to where I sat, put her arm around me, and hugged. I smelled the high floral note of her cologne.

"Two murder cases in one week," she said. "I haven't had this much fun in years."

I punched her arm.

A few minutes later, Ben came back in. He carried my sweatshirt.

"Thanks," I said, reaching for it.

"It's as much for me as it is for you." His eyes slid down, then up again. "I don't need any . . . distractions."

I slipped the sweatshirt over my head.

What followed was an hour-long grilling session. Ben put forth a scenario of self-defense, then one of passionate anger.

Charlene interrupted any questions about my relationship with Ronnie, the Egyptian, or our breakup. "She can't answer that," she said to almost every question.

Ben turned to me. "If you did this, confess now, before we find more evidence. It'll go a lot easier on you."

Charlene stood up. "Ben, stop it. You have the facts. Leave her alone."

Ben's mouth pulled into a tight line. The muscle in his jaw worked silently. He stretched his long legs out and tossed his pen across the table. It clattered to the floor.

Just then the door opened, and two state troopers stepped into the room. Ben excused himself and followed them into the hall.

I looked at Charlene. She sat back down and raised her eyes to the bright fluorescent light hanging from its cage in the ceiling. She sighed. "The state police are finished. Now, we'll have to see," she said.

"What does that mean?" I squeaked. "I didn't kill him. Can't they see that? Why would I show Ben if—"

"Kate." She held her palms up and spread her fingers wide. "We'll just have to see what they say."

After a few tense moments, Ben came back in.

"We just finished searching your place," he said.

I opened my mouth to speak, but Charlene interrupted. "I've got Ernie. He's with Marci."

"That's good," I managed. It wouldn't help my case if Ernie chomped on any official state ankles.

Ben said, "It looks like Ronnie was killed somewhere else. So, we're letting you go . . . for now. The state boys think we caught you just before you dumped the body."

"Ben, I didn't—"

He cut me off. "Look, I get it, okay? I'll do my best to find anyone else that would want Ronnie dead."

I got up to leave.

"Kate?" Ben said.

I turned.

"Charlene told me about the theatre and Taz. The state police saw the stage. They said it's pretty bad."

I stood where I was. I felt exposed and, after the last hour of interrogation, raw.

"I'll look into that angle." Ben bent and picked up his pen. "And for what it's worth," he straightened and looked me in the eye, "I'm sorry."

Sorry for what? The theatre? Ronnie? Dumping me without a word half a lifetime ago?

I did a small nod and walked out behind Charlene.

* * *

In the hall, Charlene and I passed the two state police troopers. They glared at me. Both emitted brainwaves that Ben Williamson had just set a homicidal maniac free to roam the streets in her pj's.

When we were almost to the door, Charlene paused. She looked around, held my elbows, met my eyes, and whispered, "I never said this, okay? You're going to have to figure this out. Ronnie's body was in your trunk for a reason."

"Ben can . . ."

"Look, he's never done a murder investigation. He's been hit with two murders in less than forty-eight hours. That's why he called in the state police detectives. Hell, he even led LaDonna and her friend to believe you were a deputy."

"That was a joke," I said. "It's kind of my fault if LaDonna believes it, actually."

"Ben needs help, and he knows it. He needed it just with La-Donna's case. Now, with this, he's got political pressure, too. He's

80

in over his head." Then she muttered, "Hell, to be honest, I'm in over my head."

This did nothing for my confidence.

She held the door open for me, and I drank in the fresh air and open space with the newfound perspective of one who might soon have it taken away.

Charlene spent the ride back to town throwing out possibilities. Howard? Someone on the council? A ticked-off constituent? I spent the ride alternating between hiccupping, hyperventilating, and repeating the phrase *Holy crap, I can't do this.*

* * *

At Charlene's office, we found Ernie sitting on the floor next to Marci's desk. His nose was buried in a fast-food baked potato loaded with chili.

I turned to Charlene and lifted my gaze to the water-stained ceiling. "Chili?" I mouthed. Then I thanked Marci and asked her to please skip the chili next time.

"Kitty called here. She knows about the theatre and . . ." Marci rolled her hand in a circle, "everything."

The Mudd Lake grapevine rivaled the Internet in speed and efficiency.

"Don't worry," Marci told us. "I lied and said it looked real good for you, and you wouldn't go to prison or anything."

Charlene gave her the fisheye. "Marci, Kate is not going to prison. Okay?"

"Uh-huh."

I busied myself trying to snatch the foil potato wrapper from a stubborn Ernie. He growled and gulped it down in two bites, then he jumped on me and wagged his tail.

"How did Kitty take the news about the theatre?" I asked. "Was she upset?" I squatted and hooked Ernie's leash to his harness.

"Nuh-uh. She invited me to the opening." Marci examined her magenta nail polish. "Said she'd hold two tickets for me for the tenth."

I ran my hand over my eyes. "Give me strength."

"Oh boy," Charlene said. "You're sure gonna need it."

* * *

An hour later, I was showered and dressed in jeans, a sweater, and my new boots. I was cleaning doggie barf off the living room rug when the phone rang.

"Couldn't you have simply divorced that politician-person?" said an elderly voice. "Don't you think bludgeoning him was a bit . . . extreme?"

"Sheesh, Kitty, I did not kill Ronnie." I looked at the ceiling. A small black spider had spun a web from my light fixture to the living room curtain. "And just so you know, I never married him."

"Details," she said. "She's probably just saying she didn't kill him because her phones are tapped . . . Darling, are your phones tapped? Do you want to call us from the pay phone at the theatre?"

"My phones are not tapped and anyway, the pay phone downstairs is broken. Who's 'us'?" I shouldered my cordless, got a glass from the kitchen cupboard and my script from the coffee table. I dragged a chair over to the spider's turf.

"I'm sure if you killed him, dear, you had a very good reason," said a voice like crinkly cellophane. Verna. She must've been listening on Kitty's circa 1962 Princess phone, the bedroom extension.

"You guys, I did NOT kill Ronnie."

"Did they really condemn the Egyptian?" Verna asked.

"I'm afraid so." I trapped the spider with the glass and slid *Brigadoon* over it. "Charlene and I are working on getting it reversed."

"Is that why you killed him? The condemnation?" Verna asked. "Or was it because you caught him in the bushes with that floozy?"

"Last time, ladies. I'm not a murderer." I climbed down off the chair, cranked the window open, and dropped the spider out to the sill. I watched him form a silky line, swing into the air in a wide arc, and land on the brick ten feet down.

"And you're okay?" Kitty asked. "Roland says the stars are in a very difficult alignment for you just now."

No kidding.

"I'm just ducky," I said. "Not a killer, just ducky."

"I'm a tad disappointed, I must admit," Kitty said. "There's such a mystique about women who kill their husbands . . . but it's probably for the best. Verna and I have so much to do by the tenth without collecting for a legal defense fund and whatnot."

"I'm directing *Brigadoon*," Verna said. "It's quite a production, music and dancing and such. Your aunt will be playing Fiona."

"I can pull it off, don't you think?" Kitty said. "I'll need the right lighting, of course."

I'd read the script, and Fiona is maybe twenty years old. God himself couldn't do that with lighting. I made a note to order a boatload of dry ice. This would be a damned foggy *Brigadoon* set—if, by some miracle, it happened at all.

"So you're certain you don't need us to raise legal fees?" Kitty said. "We need to be sure, so that we know which plan to implement, A or B."

"Kitty, please don't implement any plans, okay? Verna? Don't let her implement any plans."

"Yes, dear," said Verna.

"All right," Kitty said. "It's a wrap then."

"So it's plan B?" Verna asked.

"Arrrgh! No plans! Promise me," I said. I cranked the window closed against the blustery air.

"Mmm-hmmm," Kitty said, and they hung up.

Kitty played an amateur sleuth in *Mayhem in Manhattan*. When the detective asked her to back off the investigation, she'd answered just like that, mmm-hmmm.

I bounced the receiver against my forehead until I felt better.

SIXTEEN

My Riviera languished at the impound as evidence, so at seven o'clock that night, I borrowed Charlene's car and drove to the outskirts of town and into the Buy Rite parking lot. I needed to clean out my desk. I could get my things, and at the same time have an excuse to be at Buy Rite. My real plan was to get into Ronnie's office and search it for clues.

Buy Rite Real Estate occupied the fourth floor of a nondescript brick office building nestled in a featureless industrial park. I rode the elevator up to four and put my key in the lock. It wouldn't turn.

Good old Lance Beaton, Buy Rite's Mr. Efficiency. New locks would have been his number one priority before that port-o-potty even touched down, let alone now.

I stood in the hallway and waited by the elevator for about five minutes. The number on the panel lit up at four. I slipped into the ladies' room and pushed the door open a quarter of an inch. I put my eye to the crack and peered through it.

The cleaning lady pushed her cart up to the plate glass entrance to Buy Rite. She undid the lock and wheeled through the lobby, taking a right into the conference room.

"Like clockwork," I whispered.

I eased through the entrance, scooted through Buy Rite's reception area, and slipped into the dimly lit inner sanctum. The silent maze of cubicles felt eerie and deserted.

The cold glow of a computer screen radiated from Ronnie's glass-enclosed corner office. A shadow moved, and I felt goose bumps erupt on my forearms. Lance Beaton sat behind Ronnie's desk, a stack of files piled high beside him. His fingers crawled over the keyboard. Papers overflowed from a big trash barrel outside the office door.

Ronnie'd always said Lance worked for corporate more than for him, and Buy Rite's headquarters had wasted no time getting the slot ready for a new branch manager.

Lance hadn't seen me come in, so I cut down the darkened first row of cubicles and came up the back way to my desk.

I switched on the bright fluorescent fixture that hung beneath my overhead file bins. It created a strangely eerie, glowing island in the somber sea of dim gray cubes. I loaded my ancient Darth Vader coffee cup into an empty copy paper box and followed it with pens, pencils, computer disks, and my Rolodex.

After a few minutes, my back muscles tightened up, and I smelled peppermint. I whirled around and stood nose-to-nose with Lance.

"H-hi," he said.

Cubicle farms are not exactly wide-open spaces. I took a step back in an attempt to regain a bit of personal space.

With a finger that protruded from his carpal tunnel brace, Lance pushed his unflatteringly hip, rectangular-framed glasses up the bridge of his nose. He tugged at his canary-yellow Hawaiian shirt, causing his vinyl pocket protector to droop. Casual dress had done this boy no favors.

"W-what are you doing here?" he said. "I mean—I heard they arrested you for . . . you know . . . R-R-R-Ronnie." The last word seemed to have snuck out, and Lance attempted to suffocate it with a quick gasp of minty air.

"They let me go." I moved sideways a few inches and brushed some dust off my jeans.

"I-I-I'm not sure you should be here . . . I mean . . . C-C-Corporate had me ch-change the locks . . ." He took a step toward me. He was breathing through his mouth again.

"I'm just cleaning out my desk."

"Why? I mean, h-how come they l-let you go?" He took another step forward, and his air intake sped up. Little beads of sweat formed on his upper lip.

I slid sideways around the end of my desk, behind my chair. I pulled the box over so it formed a barrier between us.

Lance pushed his glasses up again, winced at the movement of his hand, and leaned over the box.

Once more, I smelled mint. His breathing came in gasps.

I pulled my head back and peered around, hoping to see the cleaning lady. The vacuum whirred in the distance, but it didn't come any closer.

I grabbed a small, framed mirror with "See the Person Responsible for Your Success" engraved across its edge and tossed it into the box. I dropped my complimentary *Buy Rite, Where Everybody Goes Home Smiling* tote bag into the carton. I yanked open the drawers and scanned them for anything personal.

"Do you know anything about any dealings with Ronnie that weren't going so well?" I asked. "Anything about Lansdowne Condominiums?"

"Hmmm . . ." He gasped some more.

Lance was glued to my every move, checking out what was in my cardboard box, on my shelves, checking *me* out.

Where was that cleaning lady?

I shoved the box across the desk, hitting Lance in the abdomen. "Lance! Pay attention!"

He pushed his glasses up again. "Huh?"

"Do you know anybody who didn't get along with Ronnie?"

Lance pushed his glasses and said, "Everybody liked him."

That plain out wasn't true. In the eight months since I'd worked here, I got the distinct impression that Lance, himself, didn't like Ronnie too well. Nor did Ronnie like Lance. He thought Lance was a creep. He wanted him out.

I pulled a gold-dipped rose out of my desk drawer. Ronnie gave it to me after a three-hour lunch with a client. I remembered thinking at the time how beautiful it was, and how sweet he was to think of me. Now, I wondered if the lunch was with Estelle. I hesitated, then laid the rose in my box.

"What about Lansdowne? What do you know about them?"

I looked up. Lance was diddling his mechanical pencil again, watching me. He was breathing hard.

My flesh began to crawl, and I suddenly couldn't wait to take a shower.

"C-corporate wouldn't want me t-talking to you," he said.

I grabbed my carton and stepped forward. I pushed it into Lance's chest and kept up the pressure, forcing him back out of my cube.

Lance turned and headed back to Ronnie's office. I knew if I didn't pass him on my way out the door, he'd be back.

I didn't want him back.

I walked to the front and waved conspicuously as I passed Ronnie's office window.

In the hall, I pushed the elevator button. Lance. What a weird duck—no, Ronnie was right—what a creep.

I couldn't go search Ronnie's office, but I wasn't defeated. On to Plan B.

SEVENTEEN

In the parking lot, I loaded my box into the trunk, pulled the Cherokee around to the back of the building, and waited by the trash chute. Fifteen minutes passed before a load of papers and miscellaneous office garbage slid out of the chute and scattered into the large dumpster before me.

I slipped the Buy Rite tote bag over my shoulder, pulled Charlene's police-issue flashlight from under the seat, and stepped out of the car. Leaning against the door, I slid off my gorgeous Jimmy Choo's and stuffed them in the tote bag. I carefully climbed on top of the Jeep's wide white hood. The trash bin was about six feet tall and maybe twenty feet long. Except for several inches of soldered metal around the trash chute, a hinged lid covered the length of the container.

I held my breath and lifted the lid. I propped it back and played my flashlight across a mixture of papers, coffee grounds, banana peels, popcorn bags, and the occasional Styrofoam carryout box. The container reeked. I turned my head and gulped a breath. The trash stopped almost halfway up the side, and although I bent over the edge and stretched as far as I could, I couldn't reach any papers. Buy Rite's house logo smiled up at me from several documents at the far end of the bin.

"Crud," I whispered.

I straightened and sat on the container's edge, then I swung my legs over and perched on the lip. My feet dangled inside. I hesitated and tried to get used to the smell. I looked at my sheer black socks the consistency of tinted Saran Wrap. I slipped back into my boots and made a very difficult decision. I spent a moment alone with them.

"After this, I'll get you both shined. I promise."

I dropped about four feet down onto what I dearly hoped was a pile of papers. Something smooshed underneath me, and half a burrito squirted out from under my boot. I yanked my foot away and stared. It was a carryout from the cafeteria, today's special. You could count on one thing if you worked in this building: Wednesday is Burrito Day! I winced.

I worked the flashlight across the mess. The acrid smells of coffee grounds and Mexican food mingled with a more sinister, sour emanation that seemed to come directly from the dumpster walls.

"Try not to think about it," I thought, thinking about it some more.

I poked my head up and gulped a breath, then I hunched down and began to flip through papers using only my thumb and forefinger.

After about five minutes, I propped the flashlight on a foam box, rested my toes on some semi-clean, old newspapers, and eased down to my knees. I dug in with both hands.

91

Under a pile of odorific, gloppy, refried beans, I spotted half-written memos from Ronnie, doodles from his telephone pad, and finally, a few of his day planner pages.

I kept digging and located all eight weekly pages from the last two months and a bunch of other Buy Rite documents. I was glad he'd shunned the electronic organizer Buy Rite gave him.

In his neat, squarish printing, I made out meeting notes, appointments related to the golf outing. Most slots from the last week were occupied by Buy Rite employee names at half hour intervals—the corporate-mandated annual evaluations.

I flipped to the last few days. The initials "M.N." followed by a question mark were jotted in the margin for Monday. An appointment in the slot for three p.m. yesterday read "Lansdowne" and "Howard." This, I could've known without the stroll through the dumpster.

Lansdowne and Howard, first thing tomorrow. Maybe this would be easier than I thought.

I could look at all the other notes later. I stuffed everything into my tote bag and zipped it shut. Now, to get out.

I stood. I heard what sounded like a miniature earthquake somewhere deep in the walls of the building and far above my head. The rumbling grew louder as whatever was barreling down on top of me picked up speed.

Over my head, the trash chute started to vibrate. I reached for the lip of the dumpster, but it was too high, I couldn't lever myself over it. I moved as far from the chute as I could and waited.

The chute rattled, coughed, and out popped two huge, very smelly, trash bags.

The cafeteria. The bags reeked of raw onions and refried beans, but at least I wasn't buried under them. I needed to get out before more stinky surprises landed in here.

At that moment, the container shuddered, and something hit me in the head. I crumpled into the garbage as everything went black.

I was on a Tijuana street corner negotiating with a large Mexican woman. I had just about convinced her to sell me a truckload of burritos when something poked me in the arm.

My eyes fluttered open, and instantly I went blind. I squinted into the beam of a flashlight. My eyes slowly adjusted.

I was lying with my face on a garbage bag—a split-open garbage bag that contained enough salsa and fermenting refried beans to fuel the space shuttle.

I gagged, eased my way to a seated position, and rubbed my aching head. Something red was on my fingers. Blood!

I sniffed it. Salsa.

"About time you woke up," a voice said.

I jumped and stuck my hand in a pile of refried beans. The person poked me with a long wooden stick, a wicked, fang-like nail protruding from the opposite side. I scrambled backward over the trash bag to the far side of the dumpster.

"This one's spoken for," the voice said.

I peered at the shape leaning over the lip of the container. It was fully dark now. I could make out only a dim head and shoulders. The voice, deep and gravelly, sounded male. He must be standing on Charlene's shiny new hood.

I flipped my flashlight around and tried to light the person's face, but my beam was too weak. How long was I out? I wondered.

The glaring light left my eyes and for a moment everything went dark again. I saw stars, and the abrupt change from light to dark made the top of my skull throb.

The beam of light resurfaced under the chin of a caramel-skinned man with a grizzled beard and cottony white hair. He glowed like a jack-o-lantern. I'd seen him before, on weekends, poking through the dumpster behind the Acadia Building.

"Scottie Forsythe," he said.

He took a roll of duct tape from the pocket of his safari vest and taped the flashlight to the edge of the container. "Lucky I came along."

Then he fastened two large C-clamps next to the flashlight. They appeared to be tied together, about a foot apart. He tossed a mass of knotted rope over the side, and it unfurled into a short five-rung ladder between the clamps.

"Made this myself. I don't go diving without it. You could climb out on your own, but it's real troublesome. This dumpster's the worst in town. It's too deep and that danged lid has a tendency to smack folks in the skull . . . what happened to you, I reckon."

Maybe.

With that ladder, I could get out or he could get in. I got to my feet.

I slipped the tote bag over my shoulder and climbed the home-made ladder. I swung my legs over the side, pushed off, and landed with a thud beside the car.

"Thanks," I said.

I needn't have worried about Charlene's finish. Scottie wore fuzzy pink bunny slippers.

"These are handy, too." He lifted his pole and leaned it against the dumpster next to me. "Saves you from climbing in sometimes. Just reach and poke."

I did a mental scan of my body to make sure I hadn't been reached and poked.

He undid his ladder, stuffed it in a large pocket in his vest, grabbed his flashlight, and deftly hopped off the hood. He peered at me again, this time up close.

"You Kitty London's niece?"

I nodded.

"You're a dead ringer for your auntie. Lean over," he said. "Let me see that bump."

I shoved my chin into my sweater. "Maybe I should go to the emergency room," I said.

"I worked there for twenty years. They ain't gonna tell you anything I can't." He pushed my hair apart with wiry fingers.

He tilted my chin up. "Let's have a look at your eyes." He held his flashlight to my face, blinding me again.

"Pupils are the same size, reacting to light and all. I'd say, you go home, put some ice on your noggin. Try to keep the bump down. You throw up, get dizzy or anything, get your hind-end to the E.R."

I had visions of my brain puffing up like a breakfast pastry. Maybe I'd go to E.R. just to be safe. Or maybe I'd trust this street person to dole out medical advice, since the odds were excellent that Buy Rite had cancelled my health insurance.

"Thanks for helping me," I said. "I left something in the trash, it got thrown out by mistake."

"Oh, you don't have to explain. There's plenty of good stuff in trash containers. I teach a class about it at the Senior Center. They call it 'Stretching Your Social Security Dollar.'"

I rolled my neck around, trying to loosen it where it had been rammed into my shoulders. I kept my eyes on Scottie. "I think my aunt took that class."

"She did." He nodded. "Quite a woman, your aunt. Glad to see her feisty again. You and that theatre, that's all she talks about."

The top of my head began to ache.

He peered at me. "It's good for the unemployed, too; dumpster diving is."

I pushed my lips together and rubbed my smarting head.

"I'll keep that in mind."

"Got a cassette player last Thursday, trash day on the Hill. Still works. Got myself six Willie Nelson tapes, too. I love that man." He patted the dumpster. "Like I said though, this one's spoken for."

He grabbed the handle on a shopping cart. It was loaded with bottles, cans, and pieces of computer gear.

"People throw these out. Can you imagine?" He gestured to a monitor. "Got a friend, fixes them up for the grade school." He reached behind a CPU and pulled out a pair of Topsiders. He slipped on the shoes, loaded the bunnies in the cart, and started away from me.

Over his shoulder he said, "Head on home and get some ice on that bump."

I thanked him and, still a little woozy, climbed into the Cherokee. Sour cream and refried beans caked the soles of my new boots, and I reeked of Eau de Dumpster. I rolled all four windows down and cranked the air to high.

I pulled out of the parking lot under the dim bluish glow from the Buy Rite offices sign.

EIGHTEEN

Fifteen minutes later, I pulled up to the curb in front of the Egyptian. I prayed to God that the unidentifiable glop smeared over the sleeve of my black sweater and into Charlene's pristine floor mat was simply Mexican food and not some biological hazard, or even worse, something that would stain. Dampness that smelled like coffee had soaked through both knees of my jeans. My head hurt, and I had salsa and cheese matted in my hair. I looked up at my landing. If I pulled my Levi's, boots, and sweater off up there in the dark, I could just slip inside—

Then I heard a noise that turned my blood to crushed ice.

From behind the doors to the theatre, I heard pounding, then screaming, then an ungodly wailing sound. I snatched up my tote bag, shoved open the car door, and ran to the lobby entrance. With a terrible realization, I recognized the voice: Kitty! It sounded like the whole building was collapsing around her. And I could hear Ernie. He sounded like he was in pain.

My hands shook as I unlocked the front door and wrenched it open. The banging, pounding, yelling, and wheezy creaking noises all became louder, almost rhythmic.

Kitty's voice came to me in a shout of alarm.

"Go home!"

The racket seemed to be coming from the stage. I ran to the concession stand to flick on the house lights, but they were already on. I reached for a golf club and burst through the auditorium doors. I saw the stage and pulled up short.

Verna sat on the left corner of the apron squeezing the life out of a wheezy set of bagpipes. Kitty perched on a stool next to her, a large conga drum wedged between her knees. She hammered away at the taut skin with the heels of her hands.

In front of the tattered backdrop, eight elderly men stomped and clomped, hooked elbows, and swung each other in wide circles. Two others stood to the side. They banged their walkers in time to the music.

Everyone hollered, "Go home! Go home! Go home with Bonnie Jean!"

Ernie pawed Kitty's thigh, digging at her black Lycra bicycle shorts. His ears were pulled back tight. He threw his head back and like a small, sausage-shaped coyote, yodeled along with the racket.

I walked toward the stage. "What the—"

"That should do it." Kitty slapped her conga in a final rim shot. "Marvelous, Verna, don't you think?"

"Thanks, boys," Verna said. "We'll meet tomorrow in the Senior Center community room, regular time."

The ten men said their good byes to Kitty and Verna and climbed down the steps. They gave me a wide berth as they passed.

It could've been the murder—then again, it could've been the odor.

I watched them as they trooped up the aisle. Several glanced back longingly in Kitty's direction. "See you tomorrow, Kitty." "You were great." "You've still got it, Kitty."

Kitty wiggled her fingers in the direction of the auditorium doors. She blew kisses. "Ta-ta! Keep practicing those fabulous dance moves." She batted her eyelashes and flashed her smile. "I swear you're Gene Kellys, every last one of you."

I rolled my eyes.

After the doors closed behind the last one, she stood up.

To me, she said, "Verna and I are doubling up as the show-case musical talent on this number because the high school band doesn't have a bagpiper." She set the big drum on the stage. "And I like doing the drum solo. I can give it so much more flair than a regular drummer, don't you think? Did I tell you we've been taking music lessons?"

I climbed up on the stage. "It has flair, I'll say that for it." So did the pies in *Sweeney Todd*, but I wouldn't eat one.

She eyed the conga. A large, official-looking yellow sticker was slapped to the wood: Property of Mudd Lake Senior Center, DO NOT REMOVE.

"It isn't exactly de rigueur," she said. "With the right lighting though, it should work."

I looked at our Fiona. Her knobby knees poked out of her bicycle shorts, and the sleeves of her faded orange AARP t-shirt flapped around her arms. Her platinum curls were tucked under a cheetah-print Lycra turban, and she wore bright orange lipstick on her wrinkly lips.

The Egyptian was likely to be history, and I was likely to be behind bars by opening night. And "Go Home with Bonnie Jean" wasn't even a bagpipe number. I rubbed the top of my achy head.

"The drum should be fine," I said. "You guys sounded . . . really original. Honest."

Verna was having trouble getting up from the edge of the stage.

"Well, dear," Verna said. "We're using quite a bit of artistic license."

She set her bagpipes on the floor, and a tortured wheeze escaped. She patted her blue-gray curls and tugged at her nylon knee socks.

"Kate, honey, my leg's asleep. Could you help me up?"

I started across the stage. Ernie loped to me and ran his snout over my shins. He snuffled, snorted, and his nose glued itself to my denim. He followed as I walked across the boards.

"Phew!" Kitty squinched her face up and covered her nose and mouth with both hands. "Verna, don't let her near you. She's rolled in something!"

"Very funny." I pulled the traveler curtain across the stage and camouflaged the shredded backdrop.

Adjusting the Buy Rite tote bag on my shoulder, I tried not to think of the taste sensation that welled up at the back of my throat.

Verna looked over at Kitty. "Bad odors don't bother me, hon. I haven't smelled a thing since 1988."

To me, she said, "Comes in handy at the Senior Center on Thursdays—" she wrinkled her nose. "Stuffed cabbage night." She waved me forward. "Come on, dear-heart. Hoist me up."

After I'd hauled Verna's substantial bulk to her orthopedically clad feet, she picked up her bagpipes and leaned close to me; her gray brows knit together in a worried frown. She squeezed the bag.

Behind a wall of creaky sound she whispered, "It's not looking good, is it, dear? I mean for the Egyptian."

I turned so that Kitty couldn't see my face. "It'll take a miracle."

"Then that's what I'll pray for." Verna nodded as if it were a done deal.

I picked up Ernie, hooked him to the spare leash that I kept under the concession stand, and followed my two geriatric thespians through the double doors. I stayed downwind and stood by the passenger side of Verna's lemon-yellow Bug.

It took me a minute to convince Kitty to roll her window down. "Maybe you should rehearse at the Senior Center for a while, okay? Things have been so . . . strange, with the vandal and Ronnie and the condemnation and everything."

"Strange indeed. That backdrop is a bit unnerving. We'll need to paint a new one or go completely avant-garde with this production." Kitty leaned over and whispered, "If it eases your mind, I was armed. I kept our prop rifle next to me. It shoots paintballs. I'm an outstanding shot, you know. I practiced quite a bit for *Annie Get Your Gun*."

"Now, I'm really concerned," I said.

"And I'm concerned about you going to prison for bumping off your second husband," Kitty said.

"Kitty, I wasn't married—I didn't—" I began.

"Details." She waved her hand. "Anyway, I rather like thinking of it like that. It gives you some pizzazz. As long as Roland keeps assuring me you'll land on your feet."

I said an internal *give me strength*. "Just keep rehearsing over at the Center until, um, I sort things out, okay?"

"I tried to get the Grand Marquis back for roof work," Kitty said, "but he's in Las Vegas. Too bad all my other men are dead. Maybe I should date a young roofer." She got a faraway look in her green eyes. "They always have those great shoulders." She pointed to her belly. "And a washboard tummy—a twelve pack."

"Six," I said.

"Huh?"

"It's a six pack. Hold your breath," I said, and kissed her on the cheek.

She leaned her head out the car window. "It'll be okay, won't it, luv? This will all work out, don't you think? I mean, Roland says so."

Her hands, nested in her lap, had a fragile, papery look. I patted her bony shoulder.

"I'm going to talk to the town council Monday. I'm sure they'll change their minds about the theatre."

She whispered, "About the other, I wouldn't blame you if you did do it. Condemning a jewel like the Egyptian. What a stupid, silly thing for a politician to do. You should never have married him."

I opened my mouth to speak, but she winked and shot me that thousand-kilowatt grin.

As Verna pulled away from the curb, Kitty sang out the window, "Don't worry, darling! Now that we've got the choreography finished up, Verna and I, we're turning our full attention to helping you beat this horrible murder rap."

A few patrons from outside the Sometime Bar peeked in our direction and quickly looked away. I cringed and hurried into the theatre to turn out the lights and head upstairs.

Next to the entrance to the coatroom, I stopped at the Pewabic tile water fountain to rinse the awful taste out of my mouth. I turned the handle, and water dripped from it. I stepped back and looked at the fountain. Something was wrong; it seemed crooked.

I held it by the edge and wiggled it. The heavy fountain shifted, then it fell off the wall and into my arms. Ernie jerked backward on his leash, and I staggered under the fountain's enormous weight. The pipes separated, and water spewed in all directions.

I dropped to my knees. Pain shot through them as they smacked hard on the watery floor. I winced and laid the heavy fixture carefully on its back. I'd rather have broken a kneecap than that fountain. Pewabic tiles of that vintage were irreplaceable. Come to think of it, so were dirt-cheap Jimmy Choo's. I yanked off my boots and tossed them clear. Then I crawled through the spray to the spigot. I wrenched it. It squealed, and I twisted until the water stopped.

Cold water soaked through my socks as I crouched and looked at the wall. What I saw made me gasp. I scooped Ernie up and leapt toward dry ground. I hugged him tighter and peered at the gaping hole left by the fountain. The bolts were sheared off at the plaster. I stared at the wall beneath where the fountain belonged. The cover and plugs had been removed from the electrical socket. Bare wires protruded from the wall and trailed to the floor. The water had stopped a fraction of an inch from the wires.

I shut Ernie in the apartment and retrieved Charlene's flashlight from the car. I stepped back into the lobby and, being careful of the water, flipped the circuit breakers in the coatroom and cut power to the theatre. I locked the entrance door from the outside and tugged on it several times. Then on wobbly legs, I carried my poor, abused boots up the outside stairs. Once inside, I deadbolted the door behind me.

During a twenty-minute, hot-as-I-could-stand-it shower, I talked myself out of calling Ben. This was Taz's work. Taz was dead. I shouldn't bother Ben with this. Besides, if Ben didn't see me, he couldn't arrest me.

Three rounds of shampoo and half a bottle of sandalwood body lotion later, I felt a little calmer and smelled a little better. I wafted out of the bathroom on a cloud of steam. Lobster-skinned and wrapped in my white terrycloth bathrobe, I threw my smelly clothes in the wash and twisted the dial until the water came on. Then, using a damp towel, I wiped down my boots as best I could and put a little polish on them. Professional help would have to wait.

I grabbed the Häagen-Dazs tub and a spoon, and headed to the living room. I sat down cross-legged on the rug and pulled the tote bag across the coffee table. I reached inside.

"You've got to be kidding me," I said out loud.

In my hand, I held yesterday's newspapers. I dropped them on the table and gawked in disbelief. Except for my shower, the tote bag hadn't been out of my sight since I left the dumpster. It had been zipped and on my shoulder when I'd been in the theatre, even when I'd struggled with the fountain. Somebody had switched the papers while I was knocked out in the dumpster. It was the only explanation. And I knew who that somebody was.

An emotional fugue state took over and I wolfed down the entire tub of Häagen-Dazs.

Tomorrow, I needed to find Scottie Forsythe. And when I did, it wouldn't be pretty.

NINETEEN

I AWOKE AT SEVEN-THIRTY with a goose egg on my skull and a throbbing behind my eyes. I tossed back two aspirin, walked and fed Ernie, and after a pot of coffee and some peanut butter toast, called Kitty to borrow her 1974 Eldorado convertible. My car still languished at the impound—evidence."

Kitty didn't answer her phone, so I called Charlene and begged to keep the Cherokee another day.

Dressed in my favorite black cashmere sweater, clean jeans, and my Jimmy Choo's, I was armed with a plan to see Lansdowne Condominiums and then Howard Douglas. After that, I'd somehow track down Scottie Forsythe.

I opened the door to Charlene's car. One inhale and I knew if I wanted to keep my best friend, I'd better get her car detailed before she saw it—or smelled it.

I gassed the car with Lysol, rolled down all the windows, and drove out to Lansdowne. Like every other building under fifty years of age, the Lansdowne development was located well outside the Mudd Lake city limits.

I parked in front of the trailer that served as the construction office. The model home loomed behind it, a big, fat, for-sale hunk of the Homogenized American Dream.

Lansdowne Condominiums looked like regular houses, only on steroids. The difference being the whole piece of property ended up shared by all the co-owners, so no one "owned" the lots under their houses.

The rickety metal stairs clanked against the trailer siding as I climbed them. I stood at the top a second, gathering my thoughts. I'd ask to see the condo model, perhaps ask a few questions, figure out how to sneak back to the trailer, and snoop. If they seemed clean, I'd ask for a job selling condos. I really needed a job, but this last part only applied if they hadn't killed my ex-fiancé.

I gathered my courage and pulled open the door.

I froze and stopped breathing for several seconds.

Kitty and Verna sat across the desk from a surly-looking gorilla of a man. He pointed to a full-scale model of the planned development.

Verna's mouth formed an "o"-like ring of surprise. Kitty blinked a few times and clutched the arm of her chair.

I thought I recognized her outfit, a vintage number, about 1960, featuring zebra accents. Kitty'd worn it in *Dastardly Dames* when she'd played a private eye.

There was silence while the London family regrouped.

"Oh . . . Kate . . . glad you could make it. Mr. Vetter, here, is just about to show Verna and me through the model. Verna will be so glad to get your opinion, won't you?" She swiveled her head to Verna, who still looked a little like a startled goldfish.

Verna gulped air, swallowed, and bobbed her head up and down in the affirmative.

"Mr. Vetter, this is my niece, Kate. She sells real estate."

Mr. Vetter's lip twitched back, half sneer, half smile.

"I've heard of her," he said in a rumbling monotone. He stood up.

"Franz Vetter," he said. He pulled a gnawed-on cigar out of his mouth with one hand and with the other, grabbed my outstretched hand. He enclosed it in his own, which was roughly the size of a boxing glove. He pumped my hand up and down.

"Nice to meet you," I said, thinking that it wasn't.

He snuffed his cigar in an ashtray brimming with butts and ash and walked around the desk. The three of us followed him out of the trailer and to the display unit. Behind Vetter's back, I raised my eyebrows in a question and looked at Kitty. She put her finger to her lips and shook her head.

We made our way through the dull three-bedroom, two-and-a-half-bath model with its requisite soaring ceilings, attached two-car garage, and the open floor plan. It was pretty, but the place had all the character of unbaked bread dough.

Franz went into a long dissertation about the conveniences of the development.

"I need to make a phone call." I pulled my cell phone out of my purse and waved it. "I'll just step outside."

I walked around the front of the trailer and eased up the metal stairs. I pushed the door open a crack and peeked through. The desk was littered with stacks of papers. I slipped inside and sat down at it. I lifted several papers and riffled through them, looking for anything suspicious or connected to Ronnie and his confrontation with Howard.

Nothing.

I swiveled in the chair and flipped through a stack of documents and files on the credenza. At the bottom of the pile, I spotted an official-looking seal, the State of Michigan, Department of Environmental Quality. I pulled the paper out and read, "Lots numbered 63-69 Bitawasee Bluffs are deemed protected under the Wetlands Protection Act." It was a cease and desist order for any draining or development of those lots. I moved over to the scale model of the planned development. The plots were numbered. Lots 63 through 69 fronted directly to Lake Michigan, the entire lakefront section of the development.

One lakefront condo would sell for at least two to three times what one directly across the street would sell for, and, worst of all, the map showed a community marina and park planned for lots 63 and 64.

If the state was blocking these lots from development, and if this complex, like most others, was being built with O.P.M.— Other People's Money—this could put the whole operation into bankruptcy. When the O.P.'s wanted their M. back, it could be one butt-ugly situation.

And I bet Howard Douglas was the O.P.

I peeked out the window. I made out the silhouettes of Kitty, Verna, and Franz Vetter in the kitchen of the model. Still time.

I moved back to the desk and slid the drawers open one after another. Nothing.

I pulled open the center drawer. I checked the window again. The three still stood in the kitchen.

In the drawer, I spotted a desk calendar. On yesterday's date, the word "meeting" was scribbled in at three p.m. That fit. A name was scrawled next to it. I peered at the scribbles. "Douglas," of course.

There was something under the calendar. I lifted up a black vinyl corner and saw a gun.

The trailer door banged open. I let go of the calendar and jerked my head up.

A gruff voice said, "Hey! What the hell do you think you're doing?"

A tall wiry man wearing a pair of grimy carpenter pants snaked his hand across the desk and grabbed my wrist in a vise-like grip. A vicious-looking hammer hung from his belt.

A photographic image of Ronnie's blood-clotted skull flashed before me. My heart danced into my throat and began working out a complicated rumba step.

Okay, think fast, think fast, think . . .

"I was looking for a phone book."

We both looked down. Amid the pile of papers strewn over the desk, in exceptionally plain sight, a phone book lay open.

Crap. No wonder it popped into my mind.

TWENTY

"Not good enough," Carpenter Pants said.

Still clutching my wrist, he reached down with the other hand and grabbed the gun. He tucked it in his waistband and pulled his grimy t-shirt over it. Then he tugged me around the corner of the desk.

"You come with me. We're gonna go talk to Mr. Vetter."

He pulled me out through the door and yanked me down the steps, never loosening his grip.

Carpenter Pants marched me through the front entrance to the model. I heard Kitty's voice from the kitchen.

"That Edie Faye showed entirely too much gum when she laughed, looked like a horse. I don't know why they let her make so many movies. She should've gone into TV sitcoms—played opposite Mr. Ed."

Vetter's bored voice, "Really . . ."

Carpenter Pants stood in the foyer. The vise tightened around my wrist, cutting off my circulation.

"Boss!" he called.

I heard Vetter tell Kitty and Verna to take a look at the patio. A sliding door opened, then closed.

Vetter came out of the kitchen and walked toward us. "Hanson, what the . . ."

"I caught her snoopin' in your office. She was goin' through your desk drawers."

Hanson held my wrist up like I was some kind of trophy. Then he dropped it and moved beside Vetter. He pulled the gun out of his waistband and pointed it at me.

Vetter's eyes narrowed to small slits. He took a few steps forward until we stood toe-to-toe. He peered at me from behind the slits and expelled a cloud of breath so rank I could almost see it.

"Whatcha lookin' for in my office, huh?" he snarled. "So soon after your boyfriend's untimely death?"

Cold sweat dribbled down my armpits and into my bra. I began to hiccup.

Think. Please God, help me think.

"I was—*hic*—looking for leads."

"What?" Vetter glared at me.

It was lame, but I had to try.

"Leads—*hic*—I was looking for leads—names of people who—*hic*—looked at your condos. They might—*hic*—be people I could show houses to."

His eyes narrowed again, practically disappearing in the folds of his now beet-red face.

I held my breath.

"I thought you got fired," he said.

Asking for a job was pretty much out of the question, so I said, "I work for—*hic*—someone else, now."

Too late, I realized who that "someone else" had to be. There was only one competitor in real estate in town. I hiccupped again and gasped up another breath.

"Douglas? You work for Howard Douglas?" Vetter hissed. "That son of a bitch—he sent you to spy on me? You tell him he's in this as deep as I am."

Hanson wiggled the gun at me. It seemed to have grown to twice its original size.

I hiccupped at it.

"What do you want me to do, boss?" Hanson said. He used the gun barrel to push a curl away from my cheek.

I jerked my head away and fought to keep my hiccups from turning into something messier.

I pictured myself joining Jimmy Hoffa as human construction filler. A fleeting thought—I didn't want to die with the hiccups. How stupid.

Vetter held his hand up to Hanson while he decided what to do with me. He looked hard at me a minute, then shook his head. "I don't buy it. Douglas wouldn't send you. You came on your own with the two old bats."

No. The bats were here first.

We heard the sliding door open and then close. Vetter leaned in even closer.

"You're playing a very dangerous game here, missy." His acrid breath almost made me gag.

I hiccupped loudly.

Over his shoulder, in the dining room, I saw Kitty freeze. Her eyes fixed on the gun. Verna bumped up behind her. She seemed unaware of the situation.

"You go snoopin' where you don't belong," Vetter growled, "you could end up—"

He didn't finish because Kitty passed out. I should say, pretended to pass out. She hit the floor like a hundred-pound sack of ham.

Whoomp!

"Oh my stars," Verna said, patting her chest. She began the slow process of working her way down to her knees.

Hanson shoved the gun in his waistband and covered it with one swift motion.

I ran to Kitty and knelt beside her. She was flat on her back with her zebra-print pumps pointed toward the dining room chandelier.

"Kitty, are you all right?" I almost yelled. Then I hiccupped. "Speak to me."

She didn't move.

I looked up. "We need a doctor, right away," I said to Vetter. I accented "away" with a hiccup between the syllables.

Vetter and Hanson exchanged startled looks.

Kitty's feet began to twitch.

I leaned in close. "Cool it," I whispered.

The twitching stopped.

I fanned her with my hands. Kitty fluttered her eyelids and sat up. Verna, now settled on her knees, joined me, fanning with one hand and patting her own chest with the other. "Oh my stars. We need an ambulance!"

"W-what happened?" Kitty asked.

"It's all right, Auntie. Lie back down." I pushed her gently back to the floor. My hiccups seemed to have stopped.

I turned to Vetter. "Look, I'm sorry. Just let me get her out of here. She has a heart condition and . . ."

Kitty began clutching at her chest.

"My heart!" she cried and sat up again.

Kitty was in grave danger of overacting. I had to get her out of there fast. "It's *all right*!" I said, with more edge to my voice than I'd use with a real heart patient. "Stay calm!" I put my hand on her chest and shoved her down.

Kitty moaned. She twitched her feet and rolled her eyes back in her head.

"My aunt has . . . other problems, too." I leaned in close to her ear and muttered, "Theatrical apoplexy."

I glanced up in time to see a look pass between Vetter and Hanson. Hanson tapped his waistband. A question.

My hiccups started again.

Vetter shook his head no. It was just the smallest of movements, but it made my skin crawl.

He looked down at us. To me he bellowed, "Get her out of here. Now!"

Kitty sprang to her feet. I grabbed Verna's arm and Kitty's hand, gave Vetter and Hanson one last "hic," and we scuttled crab-like out the door.

TWENTY-ONE

KITTY STOOD OUTSIDE THE passenger door to the VW. Some detective—I'd walked right past it on the way in.

"That was really something, wasn't it?" Kitty grinned and rocked on her zebra heels.

I grabbed her elbow and pulled her close to me. I looked around and kept my voice low. "Kitty, these guys are dangerous. Is this Plan B? Please, no more, okay?"

"I think you need me. Did you see that performance?" She looked back at the condo. "Too bad one doesn't get reviews for this sort of thing. I was rather brilliant, don't you think?"

She rocked on her heels again and looked like she was about to crow.

I took a deep breath and faced upward. I watched the clouds rolling in. No hiccup. I looked back at Kitty. I exhaled a sigh.

"Thank you for what you did in there. That really was quick thinking."

I opened Kitty's door, and she got in.

"No more, though," I said.

I peeked around the trailer. The door to the model remained closed. I could see movement inside.

"Did you find anything, dear?" Verna dug in her big purse and produced her keys. "Did you notice the wetlands? Could they pose a problem?"

"I, um, I," I sputtered.

Verna looked up, waiting.

"Yes," I conceded. "I think they might."

"Well, good then." She shoved her key in the ignition. "We've started in the right place."

"Please. No more Plan B! If you see these guys again," I pointed to the model, "you call me right away. Okay?"

Kitty cut me a crisp salute. "Mmm-hmmm!"

The VW puttered to life.

I slid behind the wheel of the Cherokee and wrinkled my nose. The morning sun had amplified the faint echo of dumpster to a roaring symphony. I shot the floor mat with more Lysol and rolled the window down. I hung my head out the window as much as possible and put the car in gear. I eased past a black sedan that was parked too close and pulled onto the highway.

I followed Verna's VW back to the Senior Center, alternating between hanging my head out the window and checking the rearview mirror for signs of Hanson or Vetter. I watched the beetle turn into the Center's parking lot, then I pulled my cell phone out of my purse.

I dug until I found the scrap of paper with Ben's number. I drove with the phone and the paper on my lap for the next few blocks. I put them both back.

I was pretty sure I'd dipped my toe in the murky waters of something illegal when I searched the Lansdowne office. Hanson and Vetter could claim they were protecting their property. I had nothing concrete to clear myself yet, not really.

Plus, I wasn't about to go running to a man who jilted me. Especially one who had a habit of throwing me in the slammer.

An hour later, I'd switched into fresh-smelling jeans, another black sweater, and my Pumas. I stood at the sink and ate a hunk of the sharp cheddar Kitty'd given me, along with a dozen crackers. I washed it down with a bottled iced tea.

Kitty and Verna and Plan B kept sneaking around in my thoughts.

I carried a few bites of cheese over and dropped them in Ernie's dish. Then I called Joe's Sunoco and made an appointment to get Charlene's car detailed. I took Ernie down to the curb with me and waited.

Joe, himself, got out of the passenger side of the tow truck. He pocketed my check for seventy-five dollars, then he sprayed the floor mats of the Cherokee with something called "New-Car-In-A-Can." By the time he drove off, it smelled great.

I sighed, took Ernie back upstairs, grabbed my shoulder bag and leather bomber jacket, and headed out the door.

I slipped the purse in my bike basket and rode the eight blocks to Manchester House, the Federal-style mansion that Douglas Real Estate called home. I leaned my bike against the side of the building and walked inside.

After winding my way through the rabbit-warren maze of small offices, I walked down a hall and past a large room split in half by a giant two-sided bookcase, my old office. I sure hoped

Howard didn't murder Ronnie. This had been an okay job, and my job prospects were wearing thin.

I peeked through the French doors to the high-ceilinged parlor. Howard sat behind the trestle table that served as his desk. The 1855 treaty with the Ottawa and Chippewa tribes was signed on this table. His chair, an 1840s-era leather wing-back, was originally owned by the founder of Mudd Lake. Many historic American artifacts, the result of a lifetime of collecting, lined multiple shelves that hung from mocha walls. Instead of enjoying the beauty, I counted blunt object after blunt object. I tore my eyes away and knocked on the door frame.

Howard was talking on the phone. His bushy eyebrows shot up when he saw me. He hesitated, then motioned for me to come in.

I took a seat in another wing-back and admired the magnificent carved oak fireplace. Three blunt objects stood, artfully arranged, on its mantel. I waited for him to finish his call.

He hung up and ran his hand through his mane. It fluffed out from his square-jawed, high-cheekboned face, creating a Michael Douglas-meets-Albert Einstein effect.

"We never finished our conversation the other day," I said.

"True, Ronnie interrupted." He looked past me, then back to my face. "I'd say I'm sorry about what happened to him, but we both know I'd be lying."

His blue eyes were enigmatic.

I ran my hands over my shoulder bag, smoothing imaginary wrinkles in the leather. Howard could've brained Ronnie with the Remington bronze behind him, or maybe with the branding iron leaning against his absurdly expensive antique desk. There were at least fifty things in this room that could've been used to clobber my ex-fiancé. I made a mental note to pick up a can of mace.

"Howard, can I ask you something?"

He waited, saying nothing.

"At the deli, I started to ask you about my job. I was wondering . . . I mean—I'd like to come back and work here."

"You would, would you?"

I nodded, but only if he didn't kill Ronnie. I had standards, and I meant to stick to them.

"It would still be straight commission."

"No problem," I said.

Howard hesitated, then he said, "I don't mean to be insensitive, but won't it be a little hard to hold open houses from prison?"

When people say they don't mean to be insensitive, my experience is, that is exactly what they mean to be. I fought to keep my expression impassive. I started a mental ten-count and wished for one of Doctor Al's plastic bats.

I sat up straighter and looked Howard in the eye. "I don't plan to go to prison. I think the real killer will be captured," I looked pointedly around at his blunt object collection and watched his reaction, "soon."

"You can start here when they do that," Howard said. He picked up his phone again and turned in his chair, a dismissal.

"I was at Lansdowne today," I said. "I talked to your friend Franz Vetter. Nice guy."

He put the phone back on the cradle. A vein in his neck popped into view and began to pulse.

"Franz Vetter is not my friend," he said.

"I don't mean to be insensitive, but you're up to your neck out there, aren't you? You threatened Ronnie about it."

Howard's face went red, and the vein came into high relief against his neck. It strummed like a violin string. I heard the copy machine churning out papers in the hallway. Bits of office chatter drifted in.

He pointed to the French doors behind me. "Close those," he said.

I got up and pushed the doors shut, eyeing the shelf above them. This room was infested with possible murder weapons. I came back to my seat.

"Regrettably, I am involved out there. Your Ronnie not only cuckolded me with my wife; he sold the property to Lansdowne Condominiums under false pretenses. I am the primary investor. The lakefront is wetlands. Unbuildable."

He made a sweeping hand gesture that loosely translated is the old German term *kaput* or "I'm screwed blue."

"My lawyers are working on extricating me from the contract, but I may stand to lose well into the six figures."

"Howard, where were you Tuesday night?"

Howard's red face deepened to magenta. "How dare you ask me that?"

I waited. We stared each other down for several seconds. Howard leaned forward and so did I.

"If you must know—"

Voices came through the door. I made out a crinkly cellophane voice. "Wait. Don't you think we should wai—"

The French doors burst open and whacked against the walls.

I whipped my head around in time to see an ancient and very expensive-looking figurine, what looked to be a fertility goddess of some sort, sailing through the air. It crashed and shattered into smithereens on the wood floor.

Kitty and Verna stood in the wide doorway. They both stared at the clay shards.

"Whoopsy," Kitty said.

I ducked my head back around the chair.

Kitty's voice rang out through the high-ceilinged room. "Howard, I want a straight answer. Are you and those Lansdowne fellows trying to frame my niece for killing her new husband?"

I winced and looked at Howard, who stared at the broken figurine. Then his brow wrinkled, and he looked at Kitty. "What the—?"

"Shame on you! Well, you won't get away with it! We're going to find proof!"

Howard glared over my shoulder. "Kitty, you're being absurd."

"You'd better turn yourself in, you devil," Kitty said. "Save yourself from sizzling like fatback in Old Sparky."

This line came from Kitty's *Mayhem in Manhattan*, circa 1961. Michigan hasn't had a death penalty since statehood in 1846, and the closest thing we have to an electric chair is in the haunted house out by the corn maze every October. I rubbed my forehead.

Howard stood up, towering over his massive desk and over me. He pointed across my chair. "Kitty London, you and what's her name . . ."

His finger stabbed the air.

"Verna," said Verna.

"You and Verna, get out of here before I call the police." Howard's voice was getting loud.

"That's just what I did, Howard. I called the police," Kitty said. "So you can go ahead and confess. Bare your deadly, rotten apple of a soul."

Mayhem went neck and neck with the *Star Wars Monologues* for howling bad lines. I scrunched down deeper in the wing-back and waited for the doozy that came next.

Kitty didn't disappoint. "You're a cad and a scoundrel, and your wife's played you for a fool."

Howard's face turned so purple I thought his head would explode. He started around the desk.

I jumped up and made a move to block him. I heard Ben Williamson's voice and shrank back into the wing chair.

"Thanks for the tip, ladies," Ben said. "I'll take it from here."

"Okay then," Kitty said. "If you're sure we can't help any more . . . It's been quite exhilarating, like one of those reality shows on television. You go get those Lansdowne fellows, too. They're out there poking guns at people and whatnot. I had to rescue Kate and Verna. And Verna's an old woman. She can't take a lot of excitement."

I winced again. I heard Kitty and Verna's footsteps fade and disappear, replaced by the slap-slither of the copier.

"Mr. Douglas," Ben said, "I need to ask you a few questions."

Ben Williamson walked around the wing chair, saw me, and did a double take.

"Hi." I waved at him.

"Kate," Ben looked from me to Howard and back again, "what are you doing here?"

I pulled my purse in front of me and wrapped my arms around it. I raised my eyebrows and looked up. "Job interview?"

"She's been asking impertinent questions. That's what she's been doing."

Ben pursed his lips. "Uh-huh. Wait for me outside, please."

I walked past Ben and gestured to the shelves. "Lots of blunt objects," I said under my breath. "Lots."

He pointed to the doors. "Close those on the way out."

I picked my way between fragments of the priceless fertility goddess and headed outside to wait for Ben.

TWENTY-TWO

I SAT DOWN ON the front step of the brick porch and pulled my jacket around me. A half block away, the clouds sailed by the top of the lighthouse tower. The temperature must've dropped ten degrees since morning. Wind gusted and whistled through the trees. It seemed to carry the typical Michigan fall message, *Get out while you still can.* Papers and a plastic grocery bag cartwheeled across the sidewalk.

After a few minutes, I heard footsteps behind me on the porch. I got to my feet, turned around, and faced Ben. I felt short and disadvantaged and wished for heels.

"Are you arresting Howard?" I asked.

"Nope, but we'll check out his alibi." He motioned to the sidewalk. I climbed down the steps with Ben close behind.

"And we're checking out Lansdowne, too," he said. "Anything you want to tell me about that place?"

I opened my mouth, closed it again, and shook my head. I stepped around the building to get my bike.

"Let's take a walk," Ben said.

My heart started to pound. I told myself it was anger, fear of getting chewed out, fear of getting arrested, but it wasn't any of those. No way would I fall for this guy again. Fool me once and all that.

I looked at Ben. He leaned against the building with one foot propped behind him and his hands in his pockets, waiting for me. The wind played through his wavy, dark hair and his eyes, blue now, watched me as I wheeled my bike toward him. I tiptoed slightly for height.

"You're not going to arrest me again, are you?"

"Nah, I'm trying to quit." His lip curved a tiny bit into a lopsided smile and that dimple appeared. My body tingled with electricity, and my heart banged against my ribcage.

No way.

I tore my eyes away from his face and, to keep them from landing anywhere else on his body, I focused out at the surging water.

We crossed the street and walked toward the park that fronted the lighthouse. I wheeled my bike by the handlebars and looked up at the towering white brick cylinder wrapped in black, spiraling stripes.

He followed my gaze. The sun broke through the clouds and glinted briefly against the red-framed glass in the tower, making the searchlight inside appear to flash. Ben stopped walking and leaned his elbows on the stone wall.

I stopped, too.

"I know you've been to Lansdowne," Ben said. "Kitty's right, they're pretty rough customers. We're checking them out." He hesitated a beat. "I should tell you to quit nosing around—leave it to the state boys and me to get to the bottom of this, but the truth is, it couldn't hurt."

I swallowed hard and nodded. I told Ben about Howard's threat at Mama's.

Then I asked, "Do Ronnie and Taz connect, at all? I mean, it's so weird."

"No. I wondered that, too," Ben said. "We've checked bank withdrawals, deposits, phone records. Nothing."

The wind whipped my hair across my face. I pushed it away. "Kitty shouldn't have called you. She doesn't have a thing on Howard, really. Sorry."

"She's just trying to help." Ben smiled his crooked smile. "She had some pretty good information. She told me that Ronnie Balfours had a meeting with Howard Douglas and Franz Vetter at Lansdowne the day Ronnie was killed."

A sinking feeling took over in my stomach. Ben put his hand on my arm. His fingers felt warm and strong through my jacket. In spite of my plummeting stomach, my heart shifted into overdrive.

"Kate, are you okay?"

"Um, yeah. I've got to go." I turned away and climbed on my bike. That information about the Lansdowne meeting was in the stolen day planner pages. Kitty couldn't have known it any other way.

I rode a few blocks in the direction of home. My ears and fingers felt like ice. One thought dominated all the others, and I didn't like it. How had Kitty and Verna known about the appointment Ronnie had with Howard at Lansdowne? They'd been outside on the patio when I'd had the discussion with Franz Vetter and anyway, that had never been said.

I thought of Scottie Forsythe, of his friendship with Kitty.

Kitty might be a little eccentric, a little exuberant, but did she let Scottie hit me in the head hard enough to knock me out? Did she have him steal those day planner pages so that she and Verna could play detective when my life was on the line? If this were Plan B, it meant Kitty was well past eccentric. How else could she have known, though? The thought made a brittle shell form over my chest.

I stopped and turned my collar up against a cold, threatening wind. I needed to find Scottie Forsythe. Now.

I remembered Scottie saying something about Thursday being trash day on the Hill. I did a U-turn and headed in that direction.

After a frigid twenty-minute ride, I arrived at the foot of brick-paved Wycoff Hill, a subdivision of restored centennial homes on the edge of town, affluent by Mudd Lake standards.

I pedaled less than half a block up the steep incline, swore under my breath, and climbed off my seat. I trudged most of the way up the hill, pushing my bike beside me.

I peered down each side street as I passed it. Trash cans and garbage bags were still heaped by the curb—a good sign. My nose was running, and my ears throbbed from the cold. I couldn't feel my fingertips.

A block away, at the top of the hill, I spotted the shopping cart Scottie'd been pushing last night—of course, it was at the very *top* of the hill.

I groaned and climbed back on my bicycle. I pedaled, huffing and grunting the rest of the way up the hill. The cart sat in a yard on the corner of Wycoff and a small cul-de-sac.

When I reached the top, I panted out a few steamy breaths and hauled myself off my bike. I stood, then bent over with a searing pain in my side. Gasping for air, I leaned on my bicycle seat. I cursed myself for blowing off my workouts the last three months in favor of rich dinners with hizzonor.

I creaked to an upright position and propped my bike on its kickstand.

Scottie poked through his cart in front of a gingerbread-laden Victorian. He wore the same many-pocketed vest as yesterday, this time over a red turtleneck. His footgear had changed to heavy brown hiking boots.

"Oh, it's you," he said. "How's the head?"

"It hurts," I said. I sniffled.

"You want me to look at it again?" He stood up and walked toward me.

"No. I don't." I folded my arms over my chest. I tucked my fingers in my armpits, an attempt to get some feeling back. "I want to ask you a question."

"Sure." Scottie trotted toward me.

I put my face close to his and watched eyes that were a startling light amber.

"Did you hit me in the head the other night?" I asked. I scowled at him and waited.

"What?" He tugged off his leather work gloves and shoved them in his jeans pocket.

"Did you knock me out? Take my papers? Give them to Kitty?"

He furrowed his brow, then scratched his head. "What are you talking about, woman?"

"The papers I found in the dumpster, someone took them out of my tote bag. Was it you?"

I watched his eyes, his body language. I looked for any sign of a lie. I wasn't sure what those would be, but I kept looking anyway. I took a step toward him. We were nose to nose.

Scottie put his fists on his hips. He didn't back up.

"Landsakes, child, you were out colder than a ham salad sandwich when I saw you. You came to just as I was fixing to climb in and check your vitals. And what would I want with your papers? Papers don't do anything for anybody."

I expelled a somewhat raggedy breath and sniffled. I believed Scottie was telling the truth. I needed to believe it.

He turned on his heel. "Come on in. I'll fix you some hot chocolate." He glanced over his shoulder at me. "And get you a tissue. Maybe two."

"Is this your house?"

"Whose else would it be? Come on," he said without turning around.

I didn't move except for my massive paradigm shift. Then I followed him past the potted chrysanthemums and into the house.

The foyer smelled of lemon oil. Richly grained oak wainscoting reached halfway up the wall. I followed Scottie to the kitchen, mindful of the way back out in case my judgment call about him was off the mark. In the high-ceilinged parlor and dining room, we passed tall, intricately carved fireplaces and beautiful antique furnishings.

A few minutes later, I sat at his kitchen table thawing the tips of my extremities on the mug of rich, creamy hot chocolate steaming in front of me.

Scottie opened a white beadboard cabinet and pulled out a bag of miniature marshmallows. He plunked a few in my mug and then a few in his.

"So," I said looking around at the well-appointed kitchen with its high-end appliances, "this dumpster thing is more of a hobby than a necessity for you, I guess."

"More of a passion, I reckon. There's so much waste in the world," he said. "Everybody wants brand-new everything all the time in this country."

The hot chocolate warmed my stomach. Scottie sat down across from me and wrapped his hands around his mug. He wore a University of Michigan class ring.

"I try to do my part to even things out a bit. I find good things people toss out, clean them up, and get them in the hands of folks that can use them," he said. "It makes people happy and keeps the past alive. I like to think I help out some. Now, what's this about your papers?"

I told him about the Buy Rite documents being switched with newspapers sometime between my dumpster dive and my astral projection to Tijuana. "Did you see anybody else in the parking lot last night?"

He shook his head. "Nope. Nobody."

"Are you sure?" Could Kitty or Verna have gotten to my tote bag at the theatre? I didn't see how—unless they came back while I was in the shower. But the deadbolt was on, and Kitty didn't have a key. I held my breath and waited for Scottie's answer.

He paused, thinking.

"What about a geeky looking guy wearing a Hawaiian shirt?" I asked.

He put his hand up—shut his eyes. "Wait, I did see some guy, that's right. Yep, in a Hawaiian shirt. He was standing outside the back door to the building when I got there. He must've just finished a smoke. He went inside while I was unloading my cart from the pickup."

Bingo. Lance Beaton didn't smoke.

Before I left, I borrowed Scottie's phone book and looked up Lance's address. Scottie insisted I take a pair of mittens and a hat he'd trash picked. I thanked him, put them on, and coasted down the hill. I rode the mile or so to the Senior Center feeling a lot warmer than I had before.

TWENTY-THREE

I ROLLED MY BIKE into the glass vestibule and held my finger poised to buzz Kitty's apartment. I glanced into the lobby and froze.

The elevator doors on the far end of the room had just opened. Hanson and Vetter stepped out and stood in the center of the lobby, their chins jutted out. They gestured to one another in short choppy movements. It looked like they were arguing.

I squatted behind my bike and peered through the spokes.

Vetter and Hanson headed toward the common area where the community room, beauty parlor, store, and cafeteria were located. I didn't think they'd seen me.

I hit the buzzer to Kitty's apartment. No answer. I buzzed again, several times. Still nothing.

I slipped out the door and scooted with my bike around the side of the building. I yanked Scottie's mittens off my hands and reached in the basket. I rummaged through my shoulder bag until my fingers closed around the smooth, cool plastic of my cell phone.

From where I stood, I could see the entire parking lot. I leaned flat against the bricks. My breath misted in front of me as I eased along the wall. I peeked around the corner—no sign of Vetter and Hanson coming out yet. I scanned the cars. Kitty's Eldorado and Verna's yellow Bug were parked in their usual spots.

I punched Kitty's number on my speed dial. The phone rang and rang. After six rings, her answering machine kicked in. I listened to Kitty's voice doing her best Mae West. I squeezed my eyes shut and shoved from my mind any reason that would prevent Kitty from answering her phone.

I hung up and racked the nether regions of my brain for Verna's phone number. I dialed once and got a stranger. I transposed two numbers and tried again.

It sounded like I woke her up. "Hello?" said Verna in her wavery voice.

"Verna, are you all right?"

"Why yes, dear. Why—?"

I cut her off. "Just take the back stairs and let me in. I'm at the rear door."

She started to speak, but I cut her off again. "Please hurry," I said.

"If you say so. I'll do my best," Verna said. She hung up.

After one last glance at the parking lot, I rounded the corner. Near the rear exit, I stashed my bike beneath some evergreens and waited. And waited. And waited.

Just as I was about to dial Ben, the door cracked open, and Verna stuck her nose out. She was panting. "Kate, dear?"

"Verna—"

"I found your aunt on the way," Verna said between gasps. "She's been quite . . . busy."

Kitty pushed her head up next to Verna's, slipped around her, and outside next to me.

"What's going on?" she said.

I opened my mouth, but no sound came out.

Kitty'd somehow managed to dye her hair in the few hours since Lansdowne. Electric lime-green highlights framed her face. She wore matching lime-green tights, a white tunic, and her zebra pumps. She looked like an extraterrestrial Phyllis Diller.

Kitty fluffed a green-tinged curl. "Verna and I missed most of our Internet class today because of our crime fighting and whatnot, but we caught the very end. That Internet girl showed me how to do this with Kool-Aid. It's all the rage. Just took a few minutes." She fluffed again. "Kate, she's seen all my movies. My plays, too. She wants to be in the Players. She's quite young. She's got one of those tongue studs and everything. How about that?"

"That's, uh, great." I touched her hair. I was surprised it wasn't sticky. I found my voice. "Is that stuff permanent?"

"Of course not, darling, it only lasts a while; you can change colors all you want. I'm trying raspberry next, maybe orange for the show. I bet I'd look like a natural redhead . . . with the right lighting, of course."

Verna, her breath back to normal, said, "Kate, dear, pardon me for asking, but why are we down here? Does this have to do with crime solving? Was Howard arrested?"

"No, but Ben's following up." I didn't want to panic them, just to get them out of there. "Do you have your car keys?" I said to Kitty.

"Under the mat," she said.

"You guys, wait right here, okay?"

They both looked perplexed, but nodded in agreement.

I jogged around the building, pressed against the brick again, and moved to the front—still no sign of Vetter or Hanson. Maybe they'd left. Maybe they were still inside.

I sprinted to Kitty's big white Eldorado convertible. Every few seconds, I reassured myself by peeking over my shoulder at the lobby entrance. I slid behind the wheel, pulled the key from under the mat, and shoved it in the ignition.

Just then, the door to the lobby opened, and Vetter and Hanson stepped into the lot.

I turned the key over. The car wheezed at me.

"Please start, please," I pleaded with it. After a few sputtering tries, it grumbled and turned over. I slipped out of the parking lot and around back. The tires squealed as I whipped around the corner of the building.

I pulled down the ramp to the delivery entrance, left the car running, and jumped out. I called to Kitty and Verna, who stood where I'd left them behind the building.

"Come on, ladies. Let's go for a ride."

They walked toward me.

"Kate, it's cold out. I believe I'll pass," Verna said. She stopped walking and stood on the brown grass.

"We have a canasta game in an hour-and-a-half," Kitty said, but she walked to the passenger side and pulled the door open.

A black sedan eased around the corner—I recognized it from Lansdowne.

"Get in, NOW!!" I yelled. I slid behind the wheel. Kitty jumped in, and I zoomed backward across the grass to Verna. I wrenched my door open and leaned against the steering wheel.

"Get in," I hollered.

Verna turned to see the black sedan idling toward us. She bent toward me.

"Now!" I said. I grabbed her wrist and pulled.

"Oh my stars," Verna said. She dove behind me. One of her support hose rolled down to ring her ankle as she skated across the back seat on her knees.

I gunned the gas and a couple of hundred horses roared to life. We dug our way across the grassy strip, screeched onto the road, and cut off the sedan. We sped away, leaving the black car in a cloud of hefty seventies-style exhaust. I turned three or four times, weaving through side streets. Several minutes later, with no sign of anyone behind us, we slipped through an alley and out onto the highway.

"Wow, this has been quite the day, hasn't it, Verna?" Kitty said. She craned her head over the red leather seat.

Verna righted herself. She patted her ample chest. "Oh my stars," she said. "Oh my stars."

TWENTY-FOUR

I LOOKED IN THE rearview mirror. No scary black sedans had followed us to the highway. I blew out air between my lips and began to breathe normally again.

Kitty and I had nicknamed the Eldorado the Land Yacht. After a while, it had a calming effect. We glided along in our own world—a silent, chrome and metal universe that could suck little foreign cars up in its gravitational field. Too bad that sedan was big and American. I checked the rearview again.

After about ten minutes, I loosened my death grip on the steering wheel enough to dig through my purse one-handed. I pulled out the scrap of paper with Ben's number and my cell phone. I handed them to Kitty.

"Dial Ben for me, would you?"

"That's a wonderful philosophy, darling." Kitty took my phone. "Just because you ate one bad kernel, doesn't mean you swear off popcorn."

I made a face at her, but I felt heat rise up my neck and into my cheeks.

"She found two bad kernels, dear, counting her ex-husband," Verna said from the back seat. "Or do we not count them if they turn homosexual?"

"No, they count," I said. "They count." I pointed to the phone. "I just need to tell Ben about Hanson and Vetter."

"Mmm-hmmm," Kitty said. She grinned and punched buttons.

When Ben answered, I gave him a heavily edited version of the events at Lansdowne that morning. I left out getting caught tossing the trailer. I left in being held at gunpoint, and the cease and desist order from the Department of Environmental Quality, and Howard being the O.P. I told him I'd seen Hanson and Vetter at the Senior Center and that Kitty and Verna were safe with me.

After I hung up, Kitty said, "So, all this dashing about with your knickers in a pretzel? It was because Franz Vetter was driving that car!"

I nodded. Kitty glanced over the back seat at Verna. Both were silent.

I turned into Lance's apartment complex. "Look for a blue Hyundai, girls," I said.

It was close to five o'clock; I didn't think he'd be home yet. While we cruised the lot, I told them about Lance Beaton and that he'd probably taken the Buy Rite papers.

We didn't see Lance's car, so we pulled up in front of the manager's office.

"Oh, land sakes, will you look at that?" Verna pointed to the yard in front of the manager's apartment.

It looked like a yard sale, but it wasn't. The yard was completely packed with lawn ornaments: figurines, elves, plastic squirrels, flamingos, frogs, even a plastic statue of Michelangelo's David.

"Pretty tacky—" I began.

Kitty cut me off. "No, Kate, look!" She pointed at a plastic, faux-stone bridge located in the center of the yard.

"Wow. That'd be perfect," I said.

"Absolutely perfect," Verna said. "The bridge for *Brigadoon*."

I pushed open my car door. "I'll go ask if we can borrow it."

"Kate, dear?" Verna said.

I turned and looked at her. She grunted as she bent over to pull her nylon knee-high back into place, then she straightened and smoothed out the white polka dots on her navy housedress. "Are you sure?"

"You bet. Like you said, it's perfect."

"No. I mean, yes, it is perfect. But are you sure you should be the one to ask?"

I stood on the blacktop outside the car and leaned my head back inside. "What do you mean?"

Verna cleared her throat and smoothed another polka dot. "Why don't I go?"

"Huh?" I turned to Kitty, confused.

Verna stuck her head close to my ear. "Why don't I go?" she yelled.

"She's right," Kitty said. "That manager's liable to be a tad flustered if you show up—that photo in the *Eavesdropper* was rather hard to miss."

I shut my eyes and rubbed the new crease that had formed in my forehead. I'd not seen today's paper. "My picture's in the *Eavesdropper*?"

"In the story about Ronnie's murder," Kitty said. "Don't worry. I gave them the one from last Christmas. You looked smashing."

I held both hands over my face and kept rubbing.

Verna climbed out and patted my shoulder. "You two keep on investigating. I'll be right here."

I took my hands away from my face and heaved a sigh. Verna set off for the manager's door.

Kitty and I watched as a short, fifty-ish woman let Verna into the apartment.

"I'm going to take a look around," I said.

I headed toward the entrance to the next building. It held four apartments, two downstairs and two upstairs. I walked through the tiny lobby and checked the mailbox. "Beaton, 3B." I trotted upstairs to Lance's apartment. I rapped on the door, waited, then rattled the doorknob. Locked. No windows, no clues to Lance. Not even a doormat.

Back outside, I looked again for the blue Hyundai. Kitty wasn't in the car anymore; Verna wasn't back yet, so I slipped around the back of the building. I didn't see anybody in the yard, and the first floor vertical blinds were all tightly closed. I stood below Lance's balcony. It held a barbecue and one lawn chair.

I walked backward onto the grass and craned my neck. I bumped into someone and jumped sideways—Kitty.

"Yikes," I said. "You scared me." I reached out and steadied her on her wobbly heels.

"Is that one his?" She pointed.

"Yeah, I'd sure like to see inside."

She held her chin up in the air and peered at the balcony. "I think his blinds are open."

Kitty pointed a few feet away, to a brightly colored plastic slide with a castle-like tower attached to it. It stood about a head taller than either of us. "You could climb on that," she said.

I eyed it skeptically. "I don't know . . ."

Kitty grabbed it and started to tug. "C'mon, Kate." Her heels sunk into the soft grass.

"Here, I've got it." I got behind it and shoved until it was under Lance's balcony. I climbed to the roof of the plastic tower. It caved slightly, but didn't collapse.

"Keep an eye out, okay?"

"Yes, darling." Kitty stood next to the tower, her Day-Glo lime in bold relief against the red and brown plastic.

She squinted up at my butt. "Are you putting on weight?"

From on top of the tower, I glared down at her. "Meet me at the car, okay?"

"I just thought you'd like to know—you're getting kind of broad across the beam."

I continued to glare while I counted to ten. My greenish-haired aunt trotted barefoot across the lawn, her zebra pumps in hand.

"Now, don't get huffy," Kitty said over her shoulder. "You just want to stay on it as you age. I could pull some strings and get you into yoga at the Senior Center." She rounded the building.

I grabbed the bottom bar to Lance's balcony railing and peeked over it. If I stood on tiptoe, my chin was about even with the cement floor. My view was absolutely perfect if I needed to confirm that Lance was guilty of harboring dust bunnies. To confirm he was guilty of anything else, this was not so hot.

Stacks of papers lay on his coffee table. The papers might have come from my tote bag; from this angle there was no way to tell. A blue duffel bag sat by the front door next to a pair of sneakers. And, perhaps the saddest thing I'd ever seen, a giant portrait of the cast of "Friends" hung above his mantel.

I heard a sound from the apartment below—rattling. Too late, I recognized the sound of vertical blinds opening.

"Daddeeee!" wailed a small voice from below.

Thinking it would be the fastest way to go, I sat and pushed myself down the slide. My hips wedged themselves halfway down.

"Oh Jeeze," I said.

"Daddeeeee! There's a big girl stuck on my princess house!"

"It's okay! It's okay!" I said over my shoulder. I grunted and tried to push the rest of the way down. Nothing moved. "I'm just leaving." I pushed with my legs and tried to stand up. The slide held fast. I grunted again. "Sorry, little girl."

I swung my leg over the edge and tried to jump. The entire structure stuck to my hind end, and I fell to all fours. With the slide still clamped to my backside, I bucked like a donkey. I heard a pop, and the whole contraption capsized and clattered to the patio pavement.

I heard a sliding door unlock, and a male voice yelled, "Hey!"

I clambered to my feet and bolted around the side of the building. I sprinted for the parking lot at a dead run.

When I got there, Kitty was in the driver's seat with the car running. Verna sat in the back with the plastic bridge hanging out the opposite window. The passenger door stood open.

I flew past Lance's blue Hyundai, slid into the passenger seat, and slammed the door. Kitty backed out of the space just as a man with the rough dimensions of Arnold Schwarzennegger but none of his charm, rounded the building.

"Hey you! Get out of that car," he hollered. "Right now!"

"How long since you drove?" I asked Kitty.

"I can't remember," she said. "Maybe last spring?"

"Oh my stars," Verna said. She grabbed the front seat with both hands and shut her eyes.

TWENTY-FIVE

ARNOLD LOOMED UP OUTSIDE my window. He smacked the hood of the Land Yacht with the flat of his hand. "Open up, you pervert!" he yelled.

"Go!" I pointed toward the exit.

Kitty stepped on the gas. The car backfired and lurched backward. She slammed the car into gear, and we hurtled forward out of the lot.

After five hair-raising minutes of bumping over curbs and swerving over the center line with the bridge hanging out the window, I convinced Kitty to pull over and let me drive.

The car sputtered as we pulled back into traffic. Verna filled us in on her visit with Mabel Vandenbrugger, the apartment complex manager.

"Mabel's quite nice. For two tickets to opening night we can keep the bridge as long as we need it."

"Great work, Verna," I said.

Kitty bounced in her seat. "Wait 'til you hear the rest!"

"Mabel has trouble sleeping," Verna said. "She watches the Home Shopping Network at night, the same as me. She saw Lance go out about ten Tuesday night." Verna patted her polka dots and smiled at me in the rearview mirror. "Mabel was up all night Tuesday. She said Lance didn't come home until five in the morning."

I looked in the rearview at her. "She's sure?"

Verna nodded. "Yes. She's sure. It was early Wednesday he came home, during Collectible Dolls."

Kitty nodded at Verna, then turned to me. "Five to five-thirty a.m."

"Exactly," Verna said.

Ronnie was killed sometime late Tuesday, early Wednesday.

"All right, Verna! Another suspect. And a bridge for *Brigadoon*! Good work."

I reached back to shake her hand. Instead Verna slapped me five. She and Kitty high-fived each other and executed some sort of complicated senior handshake.

"Hey, how did you guys know about Ronnie's meeting with Howard and Lansdowne?" I said when they were through.

"Oh, that," Kitty said. "Tell her, Verna."

"Franz Vetter's sister lives on my floor," Verna said. "One evening at bingo, she mentioned her brother's dealings with Ronnie. Part of Plan B was for me to talk with her." She looked at Kitty. "My questioning skills are kind of rusty, but I managed."

"Verna used to work for the government," Kitty whispered, "in China."

"She means for our government, not the Chinese, dear. It was only for a short time when I was doing missionary work."

I tried to picture Verna interrogating Chinese spies. It didn't work.

"So anyhoo, I stopped by Lydia's with some cookies. She told me that she had lunch with Franz Tuesday," Verna said. "He mentioned his plan to meet with Howard and Ronnie at Lansdowne."

In the rearview, I watched our frumpy Mata Hari fiddle with her support hose.

"Wow," I said. "You're really something."

"Hey, what am I? Cod liver?" Kitty said.

"Chopped," I said.

"Huh?"

Even though Vetter and Hanson may have had a legitimate reason to be at the Senior Center, they were still dangerous suspects, so I walked Kitty and Verna inside and checked their apartments.

I stood in Kitty's foyer and rubbed the urn that contained the collective ashes of the Oldsmobile, the Plymouth, and the Town Car. Kitty'd consolidated all of her dead husbands to save space. We'd taken to rubbing them for good luck.

"Can I borrow the Land Yacht?" I asked.

"Certainly, darling." Kitty kicked off her shoes and yawned. She plunked onto a yellow satin chaise below a framed poster: *Housewives from Outerspace*—a curvaceous thirty-year-old Kitty in a foil spacesuit caught vacuuming a floating rug.

"I think Verna and I are taking tomorrow off from investigating. What with Howard and Vetter and Lance and whatnot, you have suspects enough to keep you busy. Besides, she's beat."

I smiled. Kitty didn't look too chipper herself, although it could have been the green hair. I remembered passing Lance's Hyundai in the apartment building parking lot.

"Was anyone else around when you got to the Land Yacht?"

"Some young man helped us load the bridge in the car," she said. "Poor fellow, nice enough, but he stuttered something terrible."

I shivered. "Kitty, that was Lance."

"Oh." She perked up. "If we'd only known, we could have captured him—Verna's just getting warmed up to intrigue and whatnot again."

I sighed and pulled her close for a hug. "Taking a day off is a very good idea."

I made her promise that she and Verna would stay in their apartments tonight and check in with each other and with me. I said good night.

On the way out of the building, I retrieved my bike from the shrubs and loaded it in the trunk of the Land Yacht. As I drove to the theatre, I sat back and let the big car weave its calming spell around me.

When I first came to Mudd Lake, Kitty spent most of that fall taking me for drives along the lakeshore in this car. She'd dress me in my snowsuit and herself in her full-length sable. We'd fold down the convertible top and blast the heat on high. I could still picture her tooling along in her Jackie-O glasses, fur coat, and leopard head scarf. She'd rest her Bombay Sapphire martini on the car door and steer one-handed along the bluffs. I got to pick the radio stations. It might not have been P.C., but boy howdy, what a memory it made for a five-year-old. And back then I needed the distraction.

I was halfway to the theatre when a loud explosion came from behind the car. Not from behind the car.

From the car.

I looked in the rearview and through the twilight saw a cloud of black smoke.

At first, I thought it was normal—a backfire or something, but there was a lot of black smoke—a whole lot. It billowed out in a cloud behind me, and it kept coming.

A truck crawled along in front of me, and a minivan carrying what looked to be a soccer team of ten-year-old boys tailgated me through the black smoke.

Lance had been around the car, and so had Vetter and Hanson. I knew nothing about bombs, but if I had one on board, that van full of kids was following entirely too close for me to avoid blowing up on it.

The Land Yacht began to sputter. I gripped the steering wheel and glanced at the billowing smoke in the rearview.

There wasn't enough shoulder to pull off. I kept my foot steady on the gas. I stuck my head out the window and waved the air behind me.

"Get back," I yelled.

One of the kids in the minivan pointed at the Land Yacht and laughed.

There was a loud blast, a thudding sound, and the car jerked to a stop. More black smoke billowed out, so thick now I couldn't see the van at all.

"Please God, let them be okay," I said aloud. I got out and jogged around the car.

The smoke had stopped, and the Land Yacht looked fine—as fine as a giant car with a bridge hanging two feet out its window can look, anyway.

I turned to the van. It appeared to be all right except for something splattered across its nose. The driver and several of the boys piled out. One of the kids bent down and peered at the van. Brown and white mush was spewed across the metal. It slipped down the sloping front end, leaving gloppy white trails.

The kid put his nose to the mush and sniffed. "Cool!" he said.

"I always wanted to see that," said another boy.

I bent over and sniffed, too. Mashed potatoes?

The first kid said, "Wow, that potato really flew out of your tailpipe, lady." He swung his arm up in an arc. "Kapowie!"

The driver, a man, glared at the globs of potato sliding down his hood. "If that had gone through my windshield, I could have been killed. I'm calling the cops."

I put my hands on my hips and started a ten-count. I got to two and said, "Do you think I did this on purpose? Do you actually think I shoved that potato up my own tailpipe? You idiot, I thought that was a bomb!"

He looked at me funny.

"Dad, we're gonna miss our game."

The boys all whined at once.

The man looked at me funny again. He kept his eyes on me. "Get in the car, kids."

They all climbed back in the van. Through the windshield, I watched as the man turned toward the boys and pointed his finger at me. He said something.

They all looked at me, serious-faced. The van backed up and pulled around me, leaving a pile of steaming potatoes on the pavement.

I got back in the car and turned the key. The car purred to life, and I sighed in relief.

A potato shoved in my tailpipe?

For some reason, this didn't feel like the work of the person who'd bludgeoned a man to death, then shoved him in my trunk.

But, I guessed it could be. Who said a murderer couldn't be hokey? And Lance was just weird enough to mix murder with hokey. I felt a chill roll up my arms.

TWENTY-SIX

MY NEAR-DEATH POTATO experience left me feeling nostalgic and philosophical. I parked in front of the Egyptian and gazed at it through the twilight.

I looked up at the dark marquee, then at Isis and Osiris and the gaudy pyramid-shaped façade. Kitty's parents, my grandparents, traveled the vaudeville circuit. In the twenties, they got the chance to hop off and build this theatre, and they took it. My apartment used to be their home.

Kitty grew up with stars in her eyes and went to New York at eighteen, to Hollywood by twenty-three. She was good, too, but the mood in Hollywood changed and buxom blondes became the thing in the sixties. She ended up back here. We drove from Chicago to visit her a lot when I was very small.

Then one day when I was five, my mom and dad went up in the sky and never came down. Two planes collided head on and vaporized in the middle of that vast airspace above the Grand Canyon. Nobody found even a toothpick.

And I came here.

Growing up in the theatre was like growing up in my own private fantasyland—a palace where the real world disappeared, and Kitty was queen, and anything could happen. Living with Kitty was so exciting, and she kept me so busy, I eventually stopped looking up at the sky.

If they demolished the theatre, or I went to jail for murder, or God forbid, both, the part of Kitty that soared above the everyday world would disappear as surely as did those planes over the Grand Canyon.

I blinked hard, fighting the dampness that insisted on coating my eyeballs. I slammed the steering wheel with my hands. Damn it, I was not going down without a fight, and neither was the Egyptian.

I rounded the side of the building and jumped. Pent-up adrenaline rushed through my blood, making my skin prickle all over. Ben Williamson sat at the top of my wooden stairs.

"Are you here to arrest me?" I took a step backward.

"Not tonight." Ben ruffled the wave in his hair with his hand. "I'm here to feed you, catch you up on things, and pick your brain."

Beside him sat two carry-out boxes from the unfortunately named yet wonderful tasting Mercury Fish and Chips. I hesitated. I hadn't tasted Mercury's fish in a decade and a half. My stomach growled. I climbed the stairs.

I stopped halfway up and squinted at Ben through the twilight. "Are you sure you're not going to use those handcuffs?"

Ben smiled his crooked smile. "Only if you want me to."

My knees wobbled, and my heart slapped against my ribcage.

"Come on, have some fish, and I'll catch you up on Vetter and Hanson."

I thought about this while the heavenly smell of a billion calories wafted down to me. My stomach growled again. I'd had more exercise today than in the last three months combined. I was ravenous.

"Oh, come on." He opened a carton and wiggled a French fry. The warm aroma of battered cod and French fries intensified and rolled through the cold air. It hooked its fingers in my nostrils and pulled me the rest of the way up the stairs.

I was very aware of Ben's warmth as I sidled around him. I unlocked the door, and we stepped inside.

A silky thread wrapped itself across my eyelashes. I brushed it away and reached for the lamp. Several black spiders, larger than the other I'd seen, hung from the ceiling and skittered across the wall.

"Sheesh, the place has been invaded," I said. "It's like something out of one of Kitty's movies."

While Ben squatted to greet an ecstatic Ernie, I got a glass and dragged my chair and script around the room. One by one, I caught each spider in the glass, climbed off the chair, and tossed it out the door.

"Looks like you need a more efficient method," Ben said, standing up.

"I know, but I hate bug spray. It's like, I don't know, genocide or something."

I was on the last spider when Ben took off his jacket and bent over to drape it across the couch. From my perch on the chair, I ogled his behind. I imagined what the backseat of that Camaro would be like today. The Eldorado would be a lot better. I could get him down there to help me get the bridge and . . .

"No!" I said. I used my training tape voice.

Ernie jerked his head toward me. He looked puzzled.

"Pardon?" Ben said.

"What?" I looked down at him and felt my face heat up. That training tape didn't work for either of us.

"Moving furniture?" Ben gestured to the yellow couch in the middle of the room.

"Kind of. I got stalled." I climbed off the chair and tossed the last spider out the door. I laid the script and glass on the table.

"Do you mind if we go downstairs?" Ben asked. "I haven't seen the theatre in a long time."

"Okay, do you want a beer?"

* * *

With my head in the refrigerator I rehearsed that question again; the one where I asked Ben why, all those years ago, he dropped me like a hot potato.

I shook my head over the egg carton and pickles. I shouldn't be thinking about men. If anything, I should be scanning the yellow pages for that convent, not fighting a case of the hottie-cha-chas for an ex who dumped me eons ago.

Why dredge up old disasters? I had plenty of new ones around. I grabbed two beers and headed to the living room.

Ben stood by the door. He held the food in one hand, Ernie's leash in the other. Ernie alternated between leaping into the air, yipping at Ben, and swishing his tail in wide arcs. The three of us stepped out into the windy, starlit night and walked down the stairs.

TWENTY-SEVEN

BEN HELPED ME PULL the bridge out of the Eldorado, and we carried it under the marquee. I unlocked the door and flicked on the lights. Nothing happened.

"Oh," I said. "I forgot."

"What?" Ben slid the bridge through the door.

"I had a kind of . . . wiring problem," I said. I told Ben about the fountain and the wires.

"Don't move," Ben said. He retrieved his police-issue flashlight and examined the wires.

He had me bring him my toolbox. Using electrical tape, he wrapped both wires and capped them off. Then he flipped the circuits, and the lobby was flooded with light.

Ben stood still a second.

"Wow," he said. He looked around the lobby at the decaying plaster, loose floor tiles, and the fountain lying on its side. "This place needs a lot of work."

I sighed. "I know."

I showed him the bolts on the fountain. He agreed that they'd been cut.

"I'm not exactly sure what Taz did when he broke in that day, but I'm pretty sure he did this—and the wires . . . probably before I came downstairs."

I imagined Taz slithering around the theatre while Kitty and I chatted over our Styrofoam coffee cups. I rubbed the goose bumps on my arms. They were becoming a permanent fixture.

We walked into the main auditorium and settled in the back row of seats. Ben handed me my carton and popped the top on one of the beers. He slid it over to me and opened the other one for himself.

I dug into my box. The rich smell enveloped me, and my mouth watered. I drizzled vinegar on the fries. I dipped a piece of cod in the plastic container of tartar sauce and took a bite. The crispy batter crunched and the flavor of tender white cod exploded in my mouth.

"Ohh, man. This is so-o good." I shut my eyes.

When I opened them again, Ben was watching me. His lips curved into a smile. The smile faded.

"Kate, the DA's pressuring me to make an arrest," he said. "Dr. Al called us when you missed remedial anger management. She said that you," he cleared his throat, "kind of made a death threat."

"I knew it. You're going to arrest me." I jumped up and, clutching my fish and chips carton, backed away.

"No, I'm not. I'm going to have dinner with you." He stayed put and bit into his fish.

"That was not a death threat." I sat back down and poked a French fry at him. "That was . . . venting."

"And did this venting include the phrase 'die Ronnie die, you'll never get the Egyptian'?"

I leaned back in my seat and examined the French fry. "Might have," I mumbled. "And I only missed remedial anger management because I was . . . you know . . ." I trailed off and popped the French fry in my mouth. "In jail," I said around it.

"I promised not to arrest you tonight, and I meant it. I came over because time's running out. You need to tell me what you know. Everything."

And I did. I sat back down, and between scrumptious bites of cod, I told him everything I'd learned about Lance.

"As far as I can tell, Lance cleaned out Ronnie's office, probably cleaned the computer files, hit me on the head, and stole the papers that I found in the dumpster," I said. "Plus he disappeared for the entire night Tuesday."

"Don't forget he shoved a potato in your tailpipe." He shook his head. "That doesn't sound like a murderer, more like junior high."

"Tell me about it. I'm not complaining. What if he'd done something—" Goose bumps erupted again. I rubbed them. "—worse?"

Ben took a sip from his beer. "I called the attorney general's office about the wetlands violations out at Lansdowne, but as far as I can tell, those two had alibis for Ronnie's murder. We're still checking on Howard. He claimed to be with his attorney in Detroit, but we can't reach her. He had motive, that's for sure. A couple of them, even."

I dipped a bite of cod in the dill-laced tartar sauce. "Maybe Hanson and Vetter hired it out. I mean they were really creepy at the Senior Center."

"They strike me as the kind to do their own killing, but I guess it's possible. Vetter's sister says they were at the Center trying to borrow money this afternoon."

I felt dumb for overreacting earlier, but my neck muscles relaxed a bit. "I guess maybe they didn't really *chase* us."

"I'll go see Lance first thing in the morning," Ben said. "With any luck, I'll have a warrant with me, and I'll look for those papers. Maybe they'll give us a motive."

"Don't forget to look for blunt objects," I said. I popped a bite of cod in my mouth.

Ben rolled his eyes at me.

Those eyes. I concentrated on breathing normally around the pounding in my chest.

Ben gazed at the ornate proscenium arch over the stage, at the huge inverted pyramid of stained glass that formed the chandelier, and at the blue velvet curtains. "This really is a beautiful place," he said.

"It was," I said. I dropped a French fry to the floor. Ernie gobbled it up.

"I don't know. Maybe it doesn't need that much after all."

"Take a walk with me," I said.

Ben followed me down to the stage. I pulled the traveler to the side. He stared up at the slashed and graffiti-covered backdrop and the splattered stage. He emitted a low whistle. "Wow."

"I know. This is ugly, but it won't get us torn down. The list of violations on those condemnation papers is huge, hopeless. The roof is the worst, and the lobby."

I hesitated, then I said, "LaDonna told me Taz came into some cash." I pointed at the backdrop. "What if he did this and the fountain, maybe more, for money? I still think he's tied to Ronnie somehow."

"I don't see how. There are no records of anything, no evidence of contact between Ronnie and Taz. I looked into the town council, too. Seems like a pretty amicable group. No hostility toward Ronnie, just minor everyday disagreements. They'd like this place gone, it's true, but I can't see them stooping to hire Taz." He looked at me. "It's going to be a tough sell, getting them to reverse the condemnation."

Ben walked across the stage and unhooked the rope that held the backdrop. He lowered the counterweights and sent the tattered scenery disappearing up into the fly space above the stage.

I gazed past the light battens to the enormous heights of the fly area. The damaged backdrop had faded into an innocuous-looking gray shadow.

"I didn't think you'd remember how to do that," I said.

Ben locked the rope in place, walked center stage, and faced me. "Some things are hard to remember, some things you never forget."

"That's a line from a Chris Isaak song, isn't it?" I said.

"Yeah." He walked toward me. "From 'Nothing's Changed.'"

For a long moment, we stood at looking each other in the dim light. His eyes took on a deep, almost navy hue.

I felt perspiration start to form above my upper lip. *Damn*, Perspiration Lip never happened to Julia Roberts.

"That's a very old song," I said.

"Some songs you want to hear again and again," Ben said, his voice almost a whisper.

Yeah, and get burned again and again, I thought. Careful, Kate. For once in your life, be smart. I turned away, took a deep, slow breath, and tried to get centered. I turned back again.

"Do you have a plan?" Ben picked up the paint ball rifle, walked down the steps, and put it in front of the orchestra pit. He looked up at me. "To try to save this place?"

"No."

I walked down the steps and looked into the pit. The best of the high school band was planning to play in three-and-a-half weeks. *Brigadoon* was hard music. They'd probably been practicing for months—the seniors, too.

"I can't lose this place, that's all I know. It'll kill Kitty. She's pretending it isn't happening. That none of this is happening. And other people are counting on this place coming back, too. I know I didn't kill Ronnie, so I keep telling myself that part's going to turn out okay. I have to, just to function. But this . . ." I turned to him again. "I don't know. All I can do is go to the town council and beg."

Ben put his hand on my shoulder, and I felt tears well up. I bit my lip until I tasted blood.

"Oh, crap," I said, "just crap."

"I've got to go," Ben said. "I'll go see Lance first thing tomorrow."

I nodded.

"Kate, it's going to all work out."

I nodded again, unconvinced. "Thanks for the fish."

We said good night, and not long after I climbed the stairs with Ernie and flopped face first on the bed. Fully clothed, I fell asleep.

TWENTY-EIGHT

ABOUT TEN THE NEXT morning, my phone rang.

"They're having a conga drum sale at Music Galore," Kitty said. "I talked it over with Verna, and we think I should invest in my own equipment. They're next door to Wal-Mart," she said. "Verna's resting so I'm going to drive on out there. Can I get my car back?"

I remembered a year ago, coming to get Kitty at Wal-Mart. She'd locked her keys in the car. It was running. It was also in the fire lane with two wheels parked over the curb.

"I was hoping I could use your car one more day. How about I pick you up?" I said.

"Perfect!" Kitty said. "I'm ready to go."

I pulled in front of the Senior Center and waited. Kitty popped into the passenger seat. To set off her new hair color, she wore pink harem pants, a large black t-shirt featuring a pink-and-lime-green fishing lure with the words "Bite Me," pink heart-framed sunglasses, and her fez.

"My own drum! How thrilling! I hope we can find a Scottish-looking conga."

I smiled at her and said a little prayer of thanks that she was so healthy and vibrant. Then I said a little prayer that I wouldn't have to move into the Senior Center with her.

Or into prison.

I put the car in gear.

By eleven, we were in Music Galore. Kitty spotted a conga drum skirted with red leather fringe.

"This one's quite artsy," she hauled the strap up over her shoulder, "and the fringe looks kind of Scottish, don't you think?"

The drum rested on her bony hip and reached almost to the floor behind her.

She slapped it a few times and hollered, "Go home! Go home!"

Three patrons took her advice and scooted out the door. A heavy-set kid of about twenty barreled toward us.

"Please don't play the instruments," he said.

Kitty ignored him. She lifted her sunglasses and bent to examine the drum. She slapped it one-handed. "This one has much more stage presence than the one at the Senior Center."

"Well, good," I said.

The clerk loomed behind Kitty and scowled. He looked at me, and his expression changed.

"You look really familiar," he said.

"She's been in the paper lately," Kitty started, "in conjunction with the mayor's murder and whatnot."

"No . . ." He squinted at me, then jabbed a finger at my chest. "I've seen you in movies—those Saturday afternoon horror flicks. You're Kitty London!"

Kitty whirled on him. "We're going to take this." She rammed the conga into his protruding gut.

"Oofh." His breath escaped in a bagpipe-like wheeze.

Kitty raised her scrawny neck high. "And by the way, young man, *I* am Kitty London. This is my niece. And you'd better watch yourself. She may well have killed her second husband."

After an agonizing few seconds, the clerk lugged the drum to the checkout.

Outside the music store, we loaded the drum in a shopping cart. We resembled a parade float as we wheeled in front of the Wal-Mart windows: a green-haired septuagenarian, her murderous niece, and a red-fringed conga drum go shopping.

I looked across the highway at Medication Nation Plaza. The coincidence of the two murders and Taz's break-in at the Egyptian still chewed at my brain.

"Wait here," I said.

I got the car and pulled up to the fire lane. My bicycle was still in the trunk so I loaded the drum into the back seat.

"I'll be back in half an hour," I said. I left Kitty cruising the aisles of Wal-Mart.

I drove across the highway and into the plaza. A poster hung in the window of the big discount pharmacy. "Coming soon to downtown Mudd Lake, another Medication Nation." It was followed by their slogan, *We won't quit 'til we're your corner drugstore.*

I swear the things were like mushrooms, a new one popped up in one of the surrounding towns every week. A smaller sign had been taped to the plate glass, next to the poster. "Now hiring: all positions."

Maybe I'd apply. I had a little retail management experience in my background, and my job prospects in real estate were looking bleak. Downtown, I could walk to work, if I wasn't in jail—if my home was still standing.

I pulled behind the plaza and climbed out of the car. Except for a faint chalk line where Taz's body had lain, all evidence of the crime scene had been washed away in an overnight rain shower. Riding a sudden wind gust, a discarded paper cup skittered across the meticulous chalk outline. Taz's thin-body silhouette and big hair looked like a macabre human sunflower drawn on the pavement.

The space where LaDonna's car had been parked remained empty. I walked to it and looked around.

I felt the hairs on the back of my neck snap to attention as I squatted down and scanned dark red spots on the cement. Blood? No, I was pretty sure that would have washed away. I remembered again that Taz used the same paint on LaDonna's car that he'd used on my stage and backdrop. I ran my finger across a dried spot. That's what this was.

I straightened and looked from BatCave Music's freight door, where LaDonna came out that day, to the right and the much larger loading bays and the back door to Medication Nation. To the left, I saw the door to Interior Beauty, Estelle Douglas's faux-financed interior design firm. My heart sank. There was one person I needed to talk to here. I'd been avoiding it, but I knew what I needed to do.

I hopped in the Land Yacht and pulled around to the front of the parking area. I glided into the space next to a fire-engine red Mercedes, Estelle's. Standing outside my car, I worked to bolster enough courage to walk inside.

When I pulled open the heavy door, a silent, padded cell of plush carpet and quilted-silk moiré enveloped me. I fought my way through enough plants to repopulate Costa Rica and reached the front desk.

"I need to see Estelle Douglas, please," I said.

A sleek ornamental receptionist looked me up and down. She stopped at my hair. I hadn't washed it that morning, only scrunched with a bit of gel. She glowered and moved on to my jeans, then to my black sweater. When she got to my Jimmy Choo's, she raised her immaculately arched left eyebrow until it threatened to pop off her head.

"Whom shall I say is calling?" Her voice sank into the padded wall covering, giving it a deadened sound.

I straightened my shoulders. I hoped in her next job she'd get to wear a paper hat and a hair net. Then I hoped in my next job *I* didn't get to wear a paper hat and a hair net.

I pointed my nose at the ceiling and peered down it at her. "Tell her it's a client."

Her eyes widened a bit, compounding my suspicions that they'd never seen a paying customer at Interior Beauty. She pushed back her swivel chair and disappeared through palm fronds.

I padded around on the deep, plush carpet and examined the artwork. I came to a canvas covered with bright, angry gobs and splotches. I squinted the way I had been taught in Art Appreciation 101. I turned my head so it was almost upside down.

I glanced around the room, then I lifted the canvas off its hanger, flipped it around, and hung it back up.

"So, you have an interest in art," a familiar voice said from behind me. "I understand you're unemployed. If you'd clean yourself

168

up a bit, perhaps you'd like a job. Oh, that's right, you'll probably be . . . indisposed."

I whirled around.

"I expected I'd see you sooner or later." Estelle turned on dizzyingly high stiletto heels and minced her way back through the palm fronds. "Come on," she said. She didn't turn around.

Estelle slid behind a thick glass slab balanced on wrought iron that acted as a desk. Behind her, more silk plants camouflaged the windows. Two large bronze statues stood at the back corners of the room. Behind one sat her turquoise golf bag, behind the other, an expensive-looking Bose stereo system. Price tags dangled from everything, even the plants and the desk.

Estelle's tailored gray pinstriped suit and burgundy blouse matched the throw pillows on the white leather boudoir chair where I sat. She must've changed them daily.

She shifted in her desk chair. It had a tag that read eighteen hundred dollars. She ran her hand through her mousse-laden, short red hair, then crossed her arms over her chest. "I suppose you want to talk about Ronnie."

"Among other things," I said. "Your receptionist, was she here on Monday? I wonder if she might have seen anything out back, when that man was murdered."

"We closed the office on Monday. Not a soul was here."

I watched her face. Her eyes reminded me of ones I'd seen on Animal Channel, in a jungle cat calculating the distance needed to pounce on a small gazelle.

I said, "Let's talk about Ronnie, then."

There was an awkward silence. I let it stretch out and become even more uncomfortable.

Finally, she spoke. "I'm sorry you had to see us the other day. It was inconsequential, really. I hardly knew him." She looked down at her desk. "He made a pass at me that morning. He caught me at a weak moment. I don't know what I was thinking."

I reached over and picked up her paperweight, a gold-dipped rose.

"Nice," I said. "Unusual." I tossed it back on the pile of papers. "I have one just like it."

We locked eyes.

She opened her mouth to speak and closed it again. I watched her swallow hard, but she didn't flinch or move her eyes from mine.

"All right. So?" she said.

"So . . . do you have any idea who might have wanted Ronnie dead?"

She regained her footing. "Aside from you?"

Don't let her get to you, just stick to the plan. I stared at her perfect, heart-shaped face. It was my turn not to flinch. Through clenched teeth, I said, "Aside from me."

She folded her hands on the glass slab, interlocking burgundy, dragon-lady nails. "Well, there's always Howard. Do you think I would get everything if he went to prison?" Her eyes glittered at the thought.

I felt my toes curl up in revulsion. "Howard has an alibi."

"Oh." She was silent a minute, then said, "There was one other person. His office manager, Lance somebody? He threatened Ronnie. Ronnie was concerned."

"Threatened, why?"

I looked at the price tag on my flimsy chair. Fourteen hundred.

She lifted a pencil and tapped it on the table. "Ronnie wanted to fire him but Corporate wouldn't allow it. But Ronnie had something on him. He planned to put it in his review."

"Thank you," I said.

She actually smiled, and the effect was again, coldly feline.

I got up to go.

"Too bad about your theatre," she said. "Progress, though. Always for the best, don't you think?"

"No. Not really," I said. I stopped at the door and turned toward her. "Not at all." I walked out.

When I reached the door, Estelle called to me. "Be a dear, and fix that painting, would you? If it falls, I'd hate to have to bill you for it."

I flipped the picture back around. The price tag that dangled from it said forty thousand dollars.

It looked better upside down.

TWENTY-NINE

ONCE OUTSIDE, I TOOK a deep breath of air and cleansed myself of Estelle, then I headed back across the highway to pick up Kitty.

I didn't see her outside so I parked and walked into Wal-Mart. I found Kitty in the checkout line.

In the cart she carried various household supplies plus a bright orange beach towel and matching bikini.

"End of season sale," she said. She eyed the tiny bikini. "I'm planning to start aerobics, get back in shape for next summer. If you'd like, I can see if they'll waive the age restrictions for you."

"What are those?" I said. I pointed to a pair of fluorescent red-white-and-blue-striped pajama bottoms that peeked out from under a box of laundry detergent.

She held them up. "I think these'll fit me, don't you?"

I eyed the tag. "Since when do you shop in the boys' department?"

"If I could afford it, I'd go to New York or maybe Milan," she said, "get a hold of some real haute couture again. It gets harder and harder to find clothes that reflect my true style here in Mudd Lake."

"I can see that," I said. "That hair color is kind of . . . limiting, for instance."

She ogled my standard uniform of black sweater and blue jeans, then my kitten-heeled boots. "You could use a little color yourself. You look like a cat burglar. A cat burglar with sexy feet."

I looked down at my sweater. "I like black," I said, and thought of LaDonna. I felt a pang of guilt. I wondered how she was holding up.

I walked beside Kitty into the busy parking lot.

"I should've picked up another pair of these pants for Verna." She pointed to the bag. "If this conga and bagpipe thing takes off, Verna and I might do a dance at the Senior Center. These'd make a great band costume. Really hot."

When we reached the back of the Land Yacht, I loaded Kitty's purchases into the car, and Kitty wheeled the cart toward the corral in the next lane.

* * *

"Good Godfreys! Is that who I think it is?" Kitty said. "You've got to be kidding!"

Kitty stood on tiptoe in the middle of the lane. She peered across to the far side of the next row. Cars were stopped in both directions, waiting for her. "Damn," she said under her breath.

I followed her gaze. A white-haired woman stood in front of a man with a black, bullet-shaped head. She was holding both hands up in the air.

"It's him!" Kitty said. "It's the Naked Bandit."

I felt my eyes go wide. I craned my neck to see. Wow. It really was the Naked Bandit. He wore a black knit ski mask and pointed a pink, plastic pistol at the woman and, by God, the rumors were right. He wore black Adidas. And between his ski mask and his Adidas, he was as naked as a plucked chicken.

The woman dropped her hands and began rifling through her purse. She pulled out a few bills and shoved them at him, smiling.

"Thank you," she said. She looked over at Kitty and waved.

I moaned and looked at the sky.

"That's Louise Hogue," Kitty said. "I will never hear the end of this. Well, he's not getting away with it!" She started toward them. "Grab my camera."

I recovered myself and lunged to stop her, but she'd already sidled her way between an SUV and a pickup truck. She headed straight for the Naked Bandit.

"Yoohoo, darling!" Kitty trilled. "Mr. Naked Bandit, halloo!"

She was too far ahead of me to catch her, so I let her go. I scooted back to the cart and grabbed Kitty's purse. I ran across the parking lot, digging for the camera. I caught up with Kitty at the cart corral. The Bandit was headed down the middle of the aisle, right in front of us.

The Bandit saw Kitty and froze. He swiveled and bumped into a car that had nosed up behind him in search of a parking spot. The driver's mouth hung open in surprise.

The Bandit wheeled around again and trotted a few steps, then picked up speed. He was about even with us when Kitty yelled, "Oh no, you don't! You've snubbed me for the last damn time."

She yanked a cart from the corral and shoved it hard. It rattled its way in front of the Bandit and rocked over on its side with a crash. He flew over it and sprawled on the far side. His shoulder smacked the pavement, and he grunted. His hands and knees made a scuffing noise as they scraped across the blacktop.

I winced. Then I held the camera up to my eye and snapped a picture of him on all fours.

"Great shot," Kitty said.

"Not so bad yourself," I said, and snapped another picture of him on one knee, rubbing his wrist. His hands and knees were scraped and covered with gravel.

"What's wrong with *me*??" Kitty yelled, her voice squeaked with frustration.

The Bandit struggled to get to his feet.

"I just want to know, how come you never pick *me*, huh?" she squawked at his naked, mildly hairy back. "I was in the movies, you know."

The Bandit stood, wobbled, and staggered away from us. He picked up a limping momentum as he crossed into the next lane.

Kitty turned to me, hands on her hips. "What am I, I'd like to know? Cod liver?"

"Chopped."

"Huh?" she said

"It's chopped liver," I said, watching the Bandit as he wove his way through startled traffic in front of the Wal-Mart entrance.

"Hey, do you want to join the Players?" Kitty yelled.

The Bandit broke into a limping trot.

Kitty held her fist high in the air and shook it after him. "Jerk!" she yelled.

I snapped another picture of his bare butt as it disappeared around the corner of the building.

On the way home, I said, "Kitty, do you think it's possible the Naked Bandit is someone we know? I mean, his build . . . something, looks familiar."

"He's too darned young to be anyone I was married to, that's for certain." She thought about it. "I wouldn't know him from Adam, but I know this much," she smiled, "he sure had a nice little patootie."

THIRTY

I unloaded Kitty and her drum at the Senior Center and headed for home. I wanted to call Ben Williamson and tell him what Estelle said about Lance. Turned out I didn't have to. When I got home, Ben was sitting on my landing again.

"I think Lance is our guy," he said. "I went to his door this morning. He jumped off his rear balcony and took off in his car. I've got an APB out."

Even after talking to Estelle, I still had my doubts about Lance as killer, but at least the heat was off me for the time being. Now I could concentrate on the theatre.

"Great," I said. I climbed the stairs and reached for the doorknob.

"Not great," Ben said. He pulled his cuffs from behind him and, in one swift motion, slapped one across my right wrist. "I have to take you in."

"Jeeze, Ben!" I pulled on my wrist.

I succeeded only in making the cuff tighter. Ben held fast to the other end.

"We're so close! Look, Lance is acting weird, and you haven't cleared Howard's alibi. And anyway, Estelle says Ronnie had something on Lance!"

"Kate, calm down. I'm taking you in for missing remedial anger management. Judge Reed wants to see you."

He pulled me by my cuffed wrist.

"Yeah, right!" I said and trudged down the stairs behind Ben. "You just want me to go quietly. I'll probably never see this place again." My voice caught on those words.

At the car, he pulled my other wrist behind me and cuffed it. "Kate, I'm serious. It's an hour or two at most."

He put me in the back and belted me in.

"That was cheap. That was so cheap." I fumed at him from the back seat. "You fed me and were nice to me last night just so you could arrest me today without a hassle. You built trust just so you could break it. Just like before."

He looked in the rearview. Impenetrable gray eyes bore into me. He glared silently for a long minute. "Look who's talking."

"What do you mean, look who's talking?" I made my voice into a mocking version of Ben's and bounced my head from side to side. "Let's see other people, Kate. It'll be good for us, Kate. We'll have a better relationship then, Kate. A better *marriage* then." I raised my shoulders to my ears for emphasis. "Poof, next thing I knew you were engaged."

Ben wheeled around in his seat. "*I* was engaged? How about *you* were engaged? I come back to town on Christmas break with a ring in my pocket, and you're not even here. I had to hear it from Charlene that you got engaged to Andy and moved to Chicago."

He snapped back around.

"That is so not true," I said. "Your girlfriend, Denise, called me and said you guys were engaged. I got engaged to Andy *after* that."

And what a mistake *that* was, I added silently. After ten miserable years, Andy runs off with his hypnotherapist, Lars. All that time, and suddenly he's swinging his bat for the other team. He probably never even quit smoking.

Ben swiveled his shoulders and looked at me through the mesh. He stared with his mouth hanging open. "Say that again."

"What?" I fumed some more and looked out the window.

"The part about Denise and me being engaged."

"What part about you being engaged don't you get?" I stared at Isis's headdress, a plaster moon caught between two horns.

"Kate, look at me."

I swung my head back and glared at him.

"I was never, ever engaged to anybody. I dated that girl, Denise, a few times at college. She wanted more. I wanted you, so I broke it off."

I felt my eyebrows knit together. "But she called me," I said. "Told me all about your wedding plans."

"She called you? I don't believe this." Ben shook his head. "I friggin' do not believe this. I was never engaged to Denise."

My mind reeled. Just a phone call, a chance meeting, gossip, that's all it would have taken to set the record straight. Where was that infamous Mudd Lake Grapevine when a body needed it?

"This could've only happened to me," I said.

"And me," Ben said. He turned to face forward again.

We were both quiet for a few seconds, thinking about what might have been. Ben put it into words.

"You realize if it wasn't for Denise, there's a good chance we'd have been married?"

There was a long pause. We gazed into each other's eyes for a moment.

"And divorced," we said in unison.

Ben started the engine. "Let's get you to jail."

THIRTY-ONE

"You might as well quit wearing a bra," the guard told me.

I padded along next to her in my socks, my boots having been deemed as deadly as my Maidenform. The meeting with Judge Reed was scheduled for two o'clock; I had an hour to wait.

LaDonna had redecorated the cell. I can't say it was cheery. Posters of bands I'd never heard of hung on the concrete block: Noose, The Undead, and an androgynous, evil-looking creature by the name of Bile. Everyone looked strung out and miserable, and like the only color they'd ever heard of was black.

I glanced down at my sweater and vowed to start wearing color. Hopefully not prison orange.

I looked around the cell again. At first I didn't see LaDonna, then I sucked in a sharp breath and clutched the guard's arm.

In the shadows near the corner, LaDonna hung completely upside down with her feet hooked through the top horizontal bar of the cell. She faced us, eye-level with our ankles. Her arms were locked together and folded tightly across her chest. Her straight black hair cascaded from her head and pooled on the concrete floor below. Her eyelids were closed.

"Oh my God," I said. "Is she dead?"

"Anybody's guess," the guard said.

LaDonna's eyes popped open.

I put my hand to my chest and sucked up a deep breath.

"Hey, Deputy Kate," LaDonna said. She looked up at me through the bars.

"She does that all the time," the guard said. "I think she sleeps like that—about to drive me cuckoo." She raked open the bars.

I walked over to LaDonna and leaned down. "Are you all right?"

"Oh, I'm great. This works almost as good as gravity boots," she said. She clasped the bars with both hands and unhooked her feet. "Watch out," she said. She flipped her legs out and bounced herself to an upright position.

"I see your foot's better," I said.

"Yeah, the cast came off late Wednesday." She wiggled her foot in a circle. "Feels awesome."

She followed my eyes as I looked around the cell. A stack of cosmetology books sat on a small desk. A shower curtain with, of all things, kittens on it, covered the toilet area. Bile appeared to be hunting the kitten closest to his poster.

After an awkward moment, I said, "It looks nice in here."

She looked around. "Yeah. Homey. But this thing," she looked down at her orange jumpsuit and tugged on it. "At court I get to wear street clothes, but my mom and Charlene, they said they get to pick 'em. I hope they know enough to get black."

I looked her in the eye. "LaDonna, you know I'm not a deputy, don't you?"

She hesitated. The hesitation turned into a long pause. She plucked at a piece of lint and sighed. "I know. But I thought if I kept calling you that, you'd, like, find someone else, you know? Get me off the hook for killing Taz?"

I went to my usual bunk and slumped down on it. "I've got problems of my own. You've heard that, right?"

She frowned. "Yeah. But like, Patrice, my friend from your anger management class? She said she took care of the Egyptian for you. Fixed it. So now you just have . . . the one thing. And you'll have time to help me."

I straightened and stared at her. "What did Patrice do?"

"I don't know. This was way back, like Tuesday night or something. Right after she saw you? We heard about your theatre being condemned from Sheriff Ben. Patrice, like, *loves* plays and stuff. She said she wanted to surprise you—to help you out. Didn't she tell you?"

I felt an icy chill creep up my spine. Was Patrice crazy enough to get rid of Ronnie thinking it would save the Egyptian? If she somehow got interrupted, she could've stashed his body in my trunk.

Maybe she "helped" LaDonna, too. Patrice said she'd been at BatCave that day. Maybe she'd gotten rid of Taz for LaDonna, but not Taz's body. If so, the girl seriously lacked follow-through.

LaDonna picked up a cosmetology book and studied the cover. "Do you think they have cosmetology courses in prison? Would they at least let me cut hair?"

The answer to that question would have to do with scissors, razors, and knives and their related capabilities, and it would only depress her.

At two o'clock, the guard let me put my bra and boots back on, then walked me down the hall to Judge Reed. She opened the door to the chambers, and I stood looking at Charlene, Judge Reed, and a red-faced and angry Doctor Al.

Doctor Al glared at me, the knob-like bun on her head twitching violently as she swiveled her head from the door to Charlene to Judge Reed.

"Come on in, Kate," Judge Reed said.

Doctor Al sneered. "That's right, be nice to her."

Charlene and Judge Reed exchanged swift glances.

"Kate," the Judge motioned me in.

I took a tentative step into the room.

"This girl is a threat to society. She should be locked up!" Doctor Al said.

She slid her foot out so that I had to step over it. I looked at Charlene and rolled my eyes. I stepped over the foot and took a seat in a folding chair positioned between the two of them.

Dr. Al wheeled around in her seat and jabbed her knobby finger into my chest. "Nobody, but NOBODY, stands me up."

"I couldn't come. I was . . . um . . . here."

"You're in VIOLATION."

I'd thought about sending a note. The wording gave me trouble. The best I'd come up with was "Sorry, I missed anger management because the guy I was mad at was found dead in my trunk."

I hung my head. "Sorry . . ."

Dr. Al smirked at me. "You will be."

"Alice, you agreed to this," Judge Reed said. "Let's just get it handled."

"You guys made me agree," Dr. Al scowled.

"Yes," Judge Reed said, "we did."

Dr. Al muttered, "I'm charging my billable hourly rate for it then."

Judge Reed explained that starting tonight, in addition to Monday sessions of Remedial Anger Management for the next six weeks, I would also answer the crisis hotline at the hospital on Friday nights. Doctor Al would spend this evening there to train me. She added the very pregnant phrase, "Barring unavoidable circumstances."

Doctor Al glared at me. It was clear to everyone that Doctor Al would rather be dancing with my head hoisted on a turkey platter.

"She's letting you off too easy," she said.

Judge Reed ignored her.

As Charlene and I got up to leave, Doctor Al turned to the judge. "Four billable hours, right?"

Judge Reed nodded.

When we were outside the judge's chambers, Charlene said, "That wasn't so bad."

"Easy for you to say," I said. "You don't have to spend an evening with Dr. Psycho."

Charlene and I were halfway down the hall when she stopped to rummage in her big purse for her car keys.

Doctor Al popped her head out of Judge Reed's chambers and motioned for me to come back. When I got within a few feet, she stuck her face close to me and whispered, "Screw with me again, and your ass is mine."

I blinked and stumbled a step backward. Then I turned on my heel and fled back to Charlene.

"Charlene, she's crazy. She's the Son of Sam of psychiatrists." I grabbed her arm and leaned into her. "I don't want to be alone with her." I looked back to make sure she was gone. "Please. Do something!"

"You could stay in jail for the weekend or answer the crisis line," Charlene said. "Those were my choices."

"Jeeze!" I said.

Charlene raised her eyebrow and looked at me. "It could be worse. Anyway, they never get any calls."

Charlene went back to digging in her oversized purse and extracted her keys. "My car looks great. Smells really clean. Oh, I almost forgot, here." She handed me the keys to my Riviera.

I kissed my car keys and hugged Charlene. I promised to behave myself at Crisis Line.

THIRTY-TWO

A LITTLE WHILE LATER, I trudged up the outside stairs to my apartment. Lance looked like the likely suspect, but I now had serious doubts about Patrice. I still thought that the two murders tied together somehow. I wanted to sit down somewhere quiet and try to figure this thing out.

I opened the door and waited for Ernie. I didn't see him. Instead, voices drifted to me from the spare bedroom. I walked to the doorway and stopped cold. My heart stepped up its pace to a brisk trot. If I wanted those two murders connected, the girl hunched over my aunt was one of the few ways that could happen.

Kitty sat in my computer chair, and Verna occupied a folding chair next to her, their backs to me. Patrice, her hair now a boisterous shade of electric purple, leaned down and clicked a key on my keyboard.

"Guys?" I said.

"She's the one I told you about," Kitty said.

Patrice looked up. "Hi, we're just designing the playbill for *Brigadoon*."

Patrice: the theatre's little helper.

"We downloaded Kitty's pictures," she said. "You got some great shots of the Naked Bandit."

Kitty grinned. "The photos are an absolute triumph." Kitty wiggled her index finger. "You can even see his whatsy-doodle."

Patrice slid the mouse over the rubberized face of Ronnie Balfours with the slogan "Vote for Ronnie!" under his chin, my mousepad. An image of the Naked Bandit came up on my screen.

I took a step toward the computer. I looked Patrice over carefully, using my eyeballs to frisk her for possible weapons. Unless you counted a navel ring and a tongue stud, she looked clean. I didn't have much choice but to roll with the situation, so I looked at my monitor.

"Wow, nasty scrape on his knee," I said.

"You bet it is." Kitty made a withered muscle. "Self-Defense over Seventy."

Kitty beamed at me. "She's seen all my movies and everything the Mudd Lake Players' ever did."

I lifted an eyebrow. "Even *Star Wars*?"

"I thought it was kinda funny," Patrice said, still moving the mouse. "Different. I saw it twice. I filmed it."

"What a darling, darling girl." Kitty leaned toward me and whispered, "Her friend LaDonna's got a problem kind of like yours."

While Patrice put together a program for a doomed show, I ran through schemes to get Kitty and Verna out of the room. I couldn't come up with anything.

I watched Patrice. With the exception of my love life, I considered myself a pretty good judge of character. I liked her. But maybe that was just because she liked Kitty.

"Star," Kitty said. She spun the swivel chair around to face me. "That's my password: 'star.' Patrice here thought it was good idea. We're employing positive imaging and whatnot."

Ernie climbed down from the hassock where he had been curled up. Ignoring me, he stretched and walked over to Patrice. She leaned down and patted his head.

"Pretty cool little dude," she said. "Part wiener dog, huh?"

"He bites," I said.

Ernie wagged his tail and leaned into Patrice, doing his best Lassie the Wonder Dog.

I gave up. Staying within earshot, I walked out of the room and plunked myself on the couch. I pulled out a pencil and pad of paper.

I drew a stick figure with spikey hair, wrote "Taz" under it, and the word "vandal." Across the stick figure I scribbled "dead."

I drew another stick figure with a penis-shaped head, felt immediately guilty and disgusted with myself, erased the penis, and drew a house with a smiley face in its place. Underneath I wrote "Ronnie." I scribbled "dead" across the stick-like chest.

I jotted notes and made complicated diagrams. I tried to come up with scenarios connecting Taz and Ronnie and their deaths. Other than Patrice being "helpful," I got nowhere.

"Kate, dear?"

I looked up to see Verna standing in the doorway.

"May I speak with you?" Verna stepped into the room and sat next to me. "It's about Patrice," she whispered.

I laid my pad aside and turned toward her.

"Did you know her brother was sent to Jackson prison? He was involved in a car-jacking with that dead vandal," she whispered. "The vandal testified against her brother."

"Oh no!" I hissed. I jumped to my feet. "We've got to get her out of here!"

"Hush." Verna grabbed my sleeve and pulled me back down. "We don't know enough to be concerned."

I caught a movement out of the corner of my eye. A spider crawled across the front of the armoire.

"You know, your aunt is just totally and completely the most awesome person I have ever, ever met."

Verna and I both jumped.

Patrice stood in the doorway.

"I know." I hiccupped.

Patrice leaned toward us and peeped around. "Until the other day, I thought she was dead."

"Nope. Not even close," I said. My hand shook as I flipped the tablet over.

I stood up and walked toward her. Verna patted my shoulder as she passed me. "Deep breaths, dear." She headed back to the computer.

"Are you worried about this place? Because I've got a plan to help you save it. It's kind of top secret." Her tongue stud got in the way and "secret" came out all lispy: "thee-cret". "You'll just have to wait and be surprised." She grinned and wiggled her eyebrows at me. "Because if I told you, I'd have to kill you."

I took a step back.

"Like, with Ronnie dead, maybe you don't need to worry about it at all." She smiled.

I swallowed hard.

"Can I maybe, like, see the theatre?" Patrice asked.

"It's dangerous," I said.

She frowned. "You think so?"

Only for me. But this would get her away from Kitty and Verna.

I took a deep breath, supressed a hiccup, and said, "No, it's not really dangerous. Do you want to see it?"

"Yeah, that'd be awesome."

I grabbed my golf club from beside the armoire. "I'll just put this back while we're down there." I clutched my seven-iron and took Patrice down the back stairs.

I held my golf club at the ready and watched her take in the theatre.

"Man-oh-man, this is killer," she said. She walked to the costume rack, peeked in the dressing rooms with their lighted mirrors and abandoned boxes of greasepaint, and ran her hand across the closest prop shelf, touching dusty wine glasses.

She pushed at a wheelchair in the wings, left over from our unfortunately choreographed original dance review, *Heidi*. She walked to center stage.

I spied the paintball rifle near the orchestra pit. I strolled down the steps and toward it. Meanwhile, Patrice stood looking out at the auditorium. Her eyes swept from the footlights to the seating and up to the balcony.

"This is really worth saving," she whispered. "I'm glad I did what I did."

Yes. But what did she do? I used my foot to slide a bit of tarp over most of the rifle.

She and LaDonna were the only ones that had seen Taz with the robe. Could Patrice have somehow been the vandal, too? My head was swimming. I gulped back a hiccup and tightened my grip on the club.

"I've really got to go."

"Oh. Yeah, sure." She walked toward me and fingered the blue velvet. "See you at Anger Management."

I nodded and hiccupped at her. I really, really needed to find out what this girl did to get herself into anger management.

After I let Patrice out, I double-checked all the theatre locks, then I went back and checked them again. I ignored five spiders crawling across the mirror in the first dressing room and climbed the steps back to my apartment. Kitty and Verna had left. I walked downstairs again and headed next door.

* * *

"Patrice was just at my place." I paced back and forth in front of Charlene's desk. "She was going to 'fix' things for me at the Egyptian. Taz sent her brother to prison, maybe she killed him, and Ronnie found out about it. Maybe she killed Ronnie, 'cause she got started on Taz and couldn't stop."

Charlene closed the folder in front of her and pulled off her reading glasses. "Settle down. Patrice is harmless. She's a little too smart for her own good, that's all. And maybe just a little," she weaved her hand back and forth imitating a sick fish, "off kilter. You're perfectly safe with her, unless you're a computer."

"Ackkk! A hacker? Now she's a hacker? She was on my computer all afternoon!"

"Do you want her to be a killer? Because now that you mention it, that's a possibility, too."

I thought of my bank accounts, my credit cards, my Pay Pal account. My computer, that was like my wallet. No, it was better than my wallet. And if she did bad things in real life, she'd been in my place. And with Kitty. And I still didn't even have pepper spray.

Charlene pushed on her desk and rolled backward in her chair. "Even if she is a killer, I don't see any reason why she'd go after you. She likes you. Told me so herself."

I put my hands over my eyes and opened them like shutters. "That worries me even more." I walked back to my place to get ready for Dr. Al and the crisis line.

THIRTY-THREE

I ENTERED LAKEVIEW COMMUNITY Hospital and took the elevator to the basement. The Help-2-U Crisis Hotline offices were conveniently, and cheaply, and creepily, located right across from the morgue. I gulped and darted past the dark glass of the door. Ronnie and Taz were right on the other side. The medical examiner had held both bodies pending further developments. Thoughts of toe tags and freezer burn danced in my head.

Doctor Alice Parker sat at the Help-2-U desk. I peeped at her through the door.

"One more minute and she goes to jail," Doctor Al said to no one but Doctor Al.

I counted to fifty-nine and stepped inside.

"Here I am!" I chirped.

She scowled at me and growled, "Right on time."

Doctor Al demonstrated how the phones worked, showed me the script I was to follow, and gave me a guidebook to read. After we role-played for twenty minutes, I felt like jumping off a tenth-story ledge.

"I feel one of my spells coming on," Doctor Al said. She grabbed her big clinking purse and waddled out the door. She promised me she'd be right back.

"Take all the time you want," I called after her. "Take four hours," I muttered to the closed door.

I looked at the red hotline phone. I felt completely ill-equipped.

The phone rang, and I almost fell off the chair. I stared at it like it was a venomous snake. After two more rings, I snatched up the receiver.

God, don't let it be anyone who's suicidal.

My voice shook as I answered, "Help-2-U Crisis Line, how may I be of assistance?"

"K-k-k-kuh," the voice on the other end said.

"This is Help-2-U. How may I help you?"

"Th-th-th-th" was all I got in return.

Goose bumps erupted in all the familiar places. I sat bolt upright in the secretarial chair. "Lance?"

"Uh-huh," came the whispered reply.

"Lance, where are you?"

"Th-th-th . . . ."

Poor creepy Lance, even now he sounded like a stalled motorboat.

"Where are you? Are you okay? You need to turn yourself in," I said.

I hit the emergency button on the console—the one that silently connected to 9-1-1.

"He-he-he-," Lance cried in my ear. What if he was suicidal? My thoughts whirred and spun out of control. He must be. Why else would he call here? I searched frantically for my script.

At that moment, Doctor Al pulled open the door and the breeze from the movement blew my script to the floor.

In a panic, I tried to remember what it said to do.

Above all else, keep talking. Be soothing, the guidebook said. I could think of nothing to say.

"When you're down, and troubled, and you need a helping hand," I began.

"I knew we should've thrown you in jail!" Doctor Al wrenched the receiver from my grip.

"Who is this?" she shrieked.

The line went dead.

I looked at the caller ID, but didn't recognize the exchange. The emergency line was connected and flashing. I picked it up.

Doctor Al clenched her fists on either side of her head, then shook them in the air. "I leave you alone for ONE MINUTE! Look what you do!"

She glowered at me. "That does it, I need a drink." She stomped out the door.

I still held the emergency phone to my ear.

"9-1-1 operator, what's your emergency, please?" a voice said.

"I need you to connect me to Sheriff Williamson, right away."

"What is the nature of your emergency?" The woman's voice sounded as if it came out her nostrils, and there was a this-better-be-good edge to it.

"I'm at the Crisis Center. A possible murderer just called in. I think he might be suicidal."

"Are you calling about a suicide or a murder?"

"A suicidal murderer."

"Ma'am, is this a suicide? Or a murder?"

"Just get Ben Williamson, right away . . . please!"

Two long minutes later, the line lit up again. "This is Ben Williamson."

"Ben, it's Kate. I'm pretty sure Lance just called here. I think he's suicidal. Either that or maybe he wants to confess."

"What did he say?"

"Nothing. I mean, he never got any whole words out, but he didn't sound good." I gave Ben the number from the caller ID.

"This is a cell phone," he said. "There's no way we can figure out where he is."

"Can't you trace it or something?" I said.

"We haven't had a murder in fourteen years until this month. The only tracing we do here is with a paper and pencil."

"What are you going to do?"

"I think I'll call the number."

The man was brilliant.

"Call me back," I said, but he had already hung up.

The rest of my shift crawled by. What if Lance came here? What if he'd recognized my voice? What if he knew I was here all along and that was meant as a threat call, not a call for help? My head was spinning. I made a promise that if Doctor Al came back, I was going to make her give me a swig of her hooch.

About 9:30 p.m., I was jarred almost off the swivel chair by the "Wedding March" coming from my purse—my cell phone. Ronnie'd switched my ringer about a month ago. Now I found it depressing and more than a little creepy. I looked out the door to the "Morgue" sign across the hall and picked up my phone.

"We can't find him," Ben said. "I called the number, no answer. We sent people to his apartment, Buy Rite, even checked Dunkin' Donuts."

"I have a very bad feeling about this, Ben."

"Me too."

"I should have been more trained in this crisis line thing," I said.

"We'll find him," he said, and hung up.

* * *

I drove the quiet streets from the hospital to the theatre. What if Lance killed himself? I was such a loser. I stopped at the Mini-Mart and picked up a tub of Häagen-Dazs. If it was good for a dented heart, it couldn't hurt when you failed at everything you touched. I pulled up in front of the theatre. With the exception of the dim lights and faint music from the Sometime Bar at the back of the Acadia, the street was eerily deserted, and dark. Too dark.

I got out of the car and stared at the doorway to the theatre. The statue of Osiris lay toppled over on its back. A motionless shape was sprawled on the tile beneath it: a Lance-shaped shape.

THIRTY-FOUR

I walked under the dark marquee with my heart kicking in my chest like a trapped rabbit. I reached around the fallen Osiris, and my hand touched Lance's neck. His skin felt warm. I pressed my fingers against his throat hoping for a pulse. I wasn't exactly sure where to press, so I pressed everywhere. I felt nothing.

I put my shoulder into Osiris and shoved. He rolled over and both Osiris and Lance lay on their backs, staring sightless at the black sky.

On the tile near Lance's hand, I spotted an empty pill bottle. I stuck my finger inside it and lifted it up. Squinting through the dim light, I made out the label. Prozac.

My heart sank. Poor, poor Lance, if only I'd been able to talk to him. If only he'd been able to talk to me, to tell me what he wanted. He was a creep and a possible murderer, but still, maybe this could have been avoided.

I fumbled through my purse for my cell phone and punched 9-1-1.

"I'm calling to report—" My vocal chords seemed to have un-plugged themselves mid-sentence. I swallowed hard and gulped a breath. "—I think . . . a suicide."

The nasally voice stiffened with suspicion. "Ma'am, didn't I speak with you earlier?"

I fought the urge to scream. "There's a body. I need to speak with Ben Williamson, right away."

"Ma'am, your sheriff is a busy man. It is a felony to harass law enforcement or to place frivolous calls to 9-1-1."

"Damn it, I need to talk to him. Now!"

She snorted. "Yeah, right." Then she hung up on me.

I got back in my car, dug out Ben's cell phone number, and di-aled it. He answered on the first ring.

"Ben, get over here quick. I'm at the theatre. Lance is here. He's—" I cleared my throat of the tears threatening to well up in-side me. "I think he's dead."

"I'll be right there." There was a pause, and I could hear radio static in the background. "The guilt probably got to him. It wasn't your fault."

"Mmm-hmmm," I said.

I sat in my passenger seat with the door open and stared, un-blinking at Lance's body. I was useless. I didn't even know CPR.

I pulled out the Häagen-Dazs carton, opened it, and held it to my mouth. In the few minutes it took for Ben to get there, I'd licked off the top two inches of ice cream.

Ben pulled up behind me, followed by the hook and ladder and an ambulance. I shoved the Häagen-Dazs back in the bag as the fire truck flipped on a floodlight. It washed the scene with a garish, high-noon brightness.

I wobbled out of my car and stood next to Ben. We watched as an EMS tech approached the body.

People started coming out of Mama's Sometime. They collected in a little knot twenty feet away.

"Are you all right?" Ben asked. His eyes stayed focused on the scene in front of us.

"No," I said. I blinked back tears.

The tech squatted next to Lance's body and felt for a pulse.

Ben turned to face me. "You probably couldn't do much. I think he knew we were closing in, and there was nowhere left for him to go." Ben brushed his thumb across my chin. "Is that ice cream?"

At that moment, the EMS tech called to us. "He's gone."

My stomach flipped over and tears welled up. I had a responsibility when I answered that line, a chance to stop this. I'd blown it.

Ben walked over to the tech. He bent down. "Have you checked his teeth?"

The tech looked at him, "He OD'ed. Why the hell would I check his teeth?"

Ben slipped on surgical gloves, bent down, and opened Lance's mouth. He checked Lance for deadly cavities. This was all getting to him, too.

"You know, his gums are really pink," Ben said. "Are you sure he's dead?"

The tech glared at Ben. He looked over at the bar and scanned the knot of people.

"Hey, Doc Bates, c'mere and pronounce this guy, would you?"

A stout, gray-haired man in a suit stepped toward the barricade. The floodlights glinted off the amber liquid in his glass.

"Is he breathing?"

"Nope."

"Got a pulse?"

"Nope."

The doctor took a sip of his drink. "Dead then. I'll get you paperwork tomorrow."

The tech smirked at Ben. Ben glared back.

The tech patted Lance's shirt pocket. "Hey, there's a note in here."

Ben reached for the note. He read it and walked back to where I stood. "It's a confession."

He leaned toward me so I could read it over his shoulder. There was an undercurrent, a spicy, musky smell to his skin. In search of comfort, I breathed him in.

He turned to me and arched an eyebrow. We both looked back at the scribbled note.

Ronnie knew. Others would find out. That was unacceptable.
Sincerely,
Lance

A confession tucked in Lance's shirt pocket, how tidy was that? So why did I have a sinking feeling deep in my belly—a feeling that something was very, very wrong?

Ben walked to the back of the Tahoe. A few minutes later, he came back with a plastic bag. He dropped the note inside the bag and sealed it, tearing a receipt off the top.

The cluster of bar patrons moved closer, moths attracted by the floodlights. Doctor Al stood toward the back of the crowd. She swayed back and forth holding a cocktail. I'd bet she'd bill the city for the four hours at the crisis line, and I'd bet there were witnesses that she'd been in that bar all night.

Semi-credible ones.

I caught her eye and kept it, then I beamed her a telepathic message. In case all that alcohol had interfered with her psychic antennae, I mouthed these words: *Screw with me, and your ass is mine.*

"Hey, look at this." The tech motioned Ben toward the pill bottle.

Ben squatted and peered at the label. He looked up at the tech. "Prozac? Lance committed suicide by eating all of his Prozac? Wouldn't you just get really, really cheerful or something?"

"Or something . . . like seizures," the tech said. "Possibly death. I think maybe the statue here fell on him and finished the job."

I moaned.

Ben and the tech pulled Osiris back to his standing position. Ben stuck a pencil inside the pill bottle, lifted it, and slipped it in another plastic bag, then the EMT tech zipped Lance's body into a much larger bag. A fireman wheeled a metal gurney over and parked it next to the body bag. They began to lift.

The fireman dropped his end and jumped back. "I think this body bag just kicked me."

THIRTY-FIVE

THE TECH UNZIPPED THE body bag part way and peered inside, then he ripped down the zipper, and Lance was immediately engulfed in a flurry of activity. They snaked tubes into both his arms and put an oxygen mask over his nose.

The tech paused, as they wheeled the gurney past where Ben and I stood. "I've got a pulse but it doesn't look good. We're taking him over to Lakeview Community," he said.

Lance's eyes didn't even flutter as they wheeled him past us. They lifted him into the ambulance and drove away.

We both watched the taillights disappear around the corner.

"I hope he makes it," Ben said. "But, I'm glad it's over. At least now, we have a confession. You can stop worrying."

I wasn't so sure.

* * *

The next morning, I called the hospital. Lance lived through the night. He was in a coma, his prognosis was abysmal, but at least he'd gotten this far.

Barefoot and in my t-shirt and flannel pajama bottoms, I carried a steaming cup of coffee to the spare bedroom and sat down at my computer. At least I hoped I still had a usable computer because I needed to write a killer speech and save the theatre.

Ernie trailed me into the room. He climbed to his usual spot atop the low hassock and curled into a ball.

I powered up my computer. Instead of my normal soothing blue desktop, my computer screen came up dark as midnight—almost pitch black. A small tan animated kangaroo hopped across my screen. Text scrolled in yellow behind him, "Click on Clyde for a big surprise."

I bet.

I grabbed the phone and dialed Charlene's number.

"There's some killer worm virus-y thing waiting to turn my computer into a boat anchor," I said.

Charlene's voice sounded groggy. "What?"

"Patrice was on my computer, remember? She's ruined it!" I wailed.

"Wait a sec." I heard her shift the phone. "Kate? Who-what are you talking about?"

"Patrice!"

"Oh, Patrice. What'd she do?"

"My computer has stuff on it. My screen's all screwed up. There's an animal."

I could hear Charlene running water in the background. "Is it a rabbit or a kangaroo?"

I looked again just to be sure. "A kangaroo . . . a kangaroo named Clyde."

"Go ahead and click on it."

"I am not going to click on it," I hollered. "I'll probably end up with a computer-generated STD or something."

"Trust me, if it's a kangaroo, you can click on it. Never click on her bunnies."

I filled her in on what I knew about Lance, thanked her, and hung up.

I held my breath, chased the kangaroo around my display, and caught it with my curser. I clicked.

What happened next made me exhale in a whoosh. I felt the muscles in my face stretch out into a wide grin.

First, black-and-white publicity stills from when Kitty arrived in Hollywood—a fresh-faced twenty-three-year-old kid filled the screen. God, she looked beautiful. On my best day ten years ago, I didn't even come close.

The pictures broke apart kaleidoscopically from the center. Then posters from her movies came up one at a time; they seemed to spin from a distance and come forward into view. I sat transfixed.

Last came small movie cameras alternating with tiny theatre curtains. I clicked each in succession. Video clips from several of Kitty's movies—among them *Dastardly Dames*, *Attack of the Dung Beetles*, and *Killer Housewives from Outer Space*—played, interspersed with footage of the Mudd Lake Players' versions of *The Star Wars Monologues*, *Heidi*, and *Pocahontas*.

Pocahontas was meant to be a tragedy. Everybody laughed at the wrong times, so they rolled with it. It sold out every night.

The screen faded to black, and a bagpiper marched across it; behind him a banner unfurled, "*Brigadoon*, October tenth."

I winced.

My blue desktop returned and my e-mail icon blinked. I clicked on it.

An e-mail from Patrice:

I made that for Kitty. It's going to be her web site. Let me know what you think.

If we couldn't save the theatre, at least this would please Kitty. At least she'd have something.

I e-mailed Patrice a thank-you, assured her Kitty would love the web site, and asked her to remove the *Brigadoon* part until I met with the council. Then I checked all of my online bank and credit card accounts and changed every password I had.

For about forty minutes I made notes. I tried to write a coherent argument for saving the Egyptian. I came to one conclusion. My points were all totally lame. I was going to fail.

I sighed, slipped on my jeans, and hooked Ernie's leash to his harness. We trotted downstairs. He made a beeline for Isis.

"Don't you dare pee there!" I yanked at him.

Something stuck out from behind the statue, a blue duffel bag. I knelt down, unzipped it, and pulled out a ski mask and a hot-pink squirt gun.

"I knew it," I told him.

I ran back upstairs, grabbed my purse, and headed out the door.

* * *

At the hospital, I located a nurse at the intensive care unit station and asked to see Lance.

"Are you a relative? Only relatives can see ICU patients."

I hesitated, "Yes. I'm his, uh . . . cousin."

She looked at me through narrowed eyes. She seemed to decide I was telling the truth, or at the very least harmless. She turned on her squeaky white, ergonomically correct heel and walked down the polished corridor. I followed.

We looked through the window at the motionless figure. So much machinery surrounded him; I couldn't see his face at all.

"Your cousin swallowed enough Prozac to kill a very depressed horse." She turned to me. "Normally with a criminal, they post a guard. With him, there's no need. On the off chance that he wakes up, he'll be too weak to get out of bed. It looks bad . . . sorry."

I bit the inside of my lip and nodded. "Can I ask you a question?"

"What?"

I hesitated. "Did he have scrapes on his hands and knees?"

"Hands and knees? Honey, he's probably dying. Who cares?"

"I just . . ."

She mistook my lack of a good lie for familial grief. She looked back through the window. "I don't know. If he did, they were minor."

"Can I look?"

She shrugged and pulled the door open. We walked into the room full of machinery. Lance looked tiny in a sea of white sheets, pumps, and tubes. The nurse lifted the top sheet, and we both peered beneath it. His gown was hiked up. Tubes snaked in and out of every orifice on his entire body except his eye sockets. The nurse lifted Lance's limp hand. An IV tube poked out of the back. She flipped the hand over.

"Yes, he does have scrapes." She pointed. "Scrapes right here." She showed me a painful looking scab that stretched across the heel of Lance's hand.

She peeked under the sheet. "His knees are skinned, too," she said.

I followed her gaze. Yep, they were. And I pretty much recognized that whatsy-doodle.

Ronnie knew. Others would find out. That was a confession of sorts, but I'd bet it wasn't a murder confession. I drove back to the theatre.

I pulled to the curb. Through my open window, I heard the twanging strains of Chris Isaak's "Wicked Game." Banging echoed through the air from the roof. I climbed out of the car and walked toward the noise.

I couldn't see anything, so I backed up into the street.

"Hey!"

I put my hand up to shield my eyes and peered toward the "Egyptian" sign on top of my building. A few seconds passed, then Ben Williamson stood up from between the legs of the giant, light-bulb-clad "Y".

I squinted at him through the glaring sunlight. Ben wore a pair of faded jeans. A white t-shirt stretched across his chest and biceps. Very big biceps. Man-oh-man, the boy sure had filled out.

"What are you doing?" I asked.

"Fixing your roof," Ben Williamson said.

My lightning-fast deductive capabilities kicked in, and I said, "Huh?"

"Fixing your roof," he repeated. "The roof leaked. I had some extra time, so I stopped by."

I squinted at him. "Are you here to arrest me?"

"Not until I finish this patch." I watched him, waiting.

He walked closer to me, over by the "E."

"Nope, no arrests today. Sorry. The district attorney is satisfied with Lance. You are officially not a suspect."

I climbed my wooden steps.

Ben dropped a hammer into a ring on the leather tool belt slung low around his hips. He came to the edge by my landing and leaned over.

"Have you ever been up here?" he asked.

I shielded my eyes again. "No."

"Just a minute," he said.

In a few seconds, he came back with a short ladder. He dropped it onto my balcony and leaned it against the roof.

"I brought this up so I could check out the roof to the fly space." He held his hand out to me. "Come on up."

When I got to the top rung, Ben grabbed my hand. His touch was warm as he helped me onto the roof. I felt that tingle of electricity.

I followed him across the gravelly surface to the corner and looked out toward Lake Michigan. The view was spectacular.

"Beautiful, isn't it."

I looked at the miles and miles of diamond-like sparkles that stretched almost to Chicago.

"My God," I said.

The lilting, flamenco of "Blue Spanish Sky" filled the air between us.

"Nice music," I said.

He smiled his little lopsided smile. "Yep, it still is. Very nice." Ben walked over to a hole in the roof and pointed. "You know, you have six or seven holes up here. It looks like most of them were drilled."

"Drilled? You mean like on purpose?" I stared at the hole.

"Yep. And this one's fresh." He pointed at it. "I'm guessing less than two days old. See the inside? The others are water stained and dirty where the rain dripped through. This one's clean. It rained Thursday night."

I bent over the opening. My mind processed the idea that someone had put holes in the Egyptian's roof. I added to it that someone had put holes in the roof *after* Taz died. Someone wanted this place gone—someone alive and kicking and skulking around Mudd Lake.

I straightened. "Ben, I don't think Lance is the killer."

Ben stared at me. "What are you talking about?"

I took a deep breath and, with the feeling I was jumping off the Egyptian roof, I told him what I knew about Lance, about the duffel, about the scrapes.

"He's the Naked Bandit. I think that's what he confessed to," I said. "He just doesn't feel right for Ronnie's murder, or even this. I still believe the two killings somehow connect. Taz and Ronnie. You said it yourself, no murders in fourteen years. Now two? And they somehow connect to the Egyptian."

THIRTY-SIX

We climbed down the ladder, then headed for my car. I lifted
the duffel out of my trunk. After we brought it back to my kitchen,
Ben pulled out the mask and the squirt gun.

"This, coupled with the scrapes, proves he's the Bandit, all
right," Ben said. "Did you see this stuff in the bottom?" He pulled
out a sheaf of papers with the Buy Rite smiley-house logo on
them.

I pulled them toward me. "These are the papers that Lance stole
out of my tote bag." I pointed to the "M.N." with a question mark.
"I'd forgotten all about that."

"Look at this." Ben handed me Ronnie's notes from the corporate
review with Lance. "Ronnie figured out that Lance was the Naked
Bandit. He was going to report him, recommend termination."

"Maybe Lance terminated Ronnie first. I've changed my mind,
he might've killed Ronnie after all." I flipped through a few more
pages.

"Nope. Couldn't have happened. We got a wire this week that the Naked Bandit struck over in Sagatoway Bluffs at midnight Tuesday. The description fits Lance, right down to his little pink squirt gun. Sagatoway is three hours away. Ronnie's time of death was between eleven p.m. Tuesday and one a.m. Wednesday morning. If Lance is the Naked Bandit, no way he could've killed Ronnie," Ben said.

"So we're back to square one."

He frowned.

"And I'm a suspect again."

Continuing to frown, he nodded.

I slapped the table. "Damn!"

"Hey . . ." Ben reached out and held one of my curls with his thumb and forefinger. He gently pulled it, and let it go. In the distance I heard Chris Isaak's deep, sugary voice singing over a rockabilly guitar riff. "We have a slew of suspects. And for what it's worth, I believe you're innocent."

When I could breathe again, I said, "Thanks."

Ben got up and walked into the living room. "Do you want this couch moved?"

I followed him. "Yeah, but it's very hard to move. Heavy chi."

"I think we can manage it."

I hesitated a minute. I walked over to the armoire. "This is the southwest corner, right?"

"Yeah, I think so." Ben looked at the sun angling in over Lake Michigan. "Yep."

"It has to go here," I said, pointing to my armoire.

To Ben's credit, he didn't ask why.

"Let's get the television out first," Ben said. He pulled the television out of the armoire and something fell to the floor. Ernie rushed in and scooped it up in his muzzle.

"Rats," I said. I headed to the kitchen and grabbed a cocktail wiener from the fridge.

Ben yelled, "Drop it."

I tossed the tiny hotdog to the floor and raised my hands. I quickly bent down and scooped up the weenie, grateful I was out of Ben's line of vision. I walked into the living room.

Ben held the turquoise glove in his hand. He dangled it in front of me. "Are you still golfing? I thought you said you gave it up."

I tossed the hotdog to Ernie. He caught it mid-air and gobbled it. "I did. Why?"

"This is a woman's golf glove."

I grabbed it from him. "Let me see that." I turned the heel of the glove inside out. "FootJoy Ladies L."

FootJoy—the same as my golf shoes. And I'd seen that color before.

"What an idiot I am. I'd just assumed this was Kitty's," I said, "part of a pair of old driving gloves. If I'd ever taken my golf glove out of the package, actually ever worn it, I would have recognized this for what it is."

Ben poked his head out from behind the armoire. "What are you talking about?"

"Estelle."

Ben raised an eyebrow and waited.

"Estelle," I said again. "I'm an idiot!"

I remembered my visit to her office, remembered the turquoise golf bag behind the bronze statue. The identical shade of turquoise to the glove I held in my hand. And she always matched.

"Ben," I flapped the glove in the air, "she was in this theatre the day Taz was killed."

Ben stepped out from behind the armoire and stared at the glove. "I never mentioned this to you, but do you know where Taz worked?"

I waited.

"He moved furniture for Estelle's company, Interior Beauty."

"My God," I said, waving the glove. "It's like the O. J. Simpson thing. She did it! It all makes sense."

"Wait. What makes sense?"

I pulled out my tablet, my complicated notes and diagrams, the stick figures of Taz and Ronnie. I jabbed at it.

"Look. Everything ties to Estelle. Taz trashed the theatre. Taz worked for her. He's dead. Ronnie had a thing with her. *He's* dead. Both Ronnie and Taz tie to the Egyptian, and the Egyptian's in trouble. Estelle's been in the Egyptian."

I stared at the page. "I can't figure out why it fits, but I know it does."

Ben looked at the diagram. He said nothing but his lips turned up into that little smile. "You love this stuff, don't you?"

"I would love it more if I weren't a suspect." I jabbed the diagram again, "And if the Egyptian weren't at stake. Another thing, Estelle wouldn't know a client if one bit her in the butt. She was paying Taz to move furniture? Can you check out the furniture deliveries, make sure they're for real? I bet they aren't. Estelle paid Taz to vandalize the Egyptian. I know it."

"Why?" Ben took the glove.

Like the O.J. thing, in the end this glove proved nothing.

"Beats the hell out of me," I said.

"I'll check this out first thing tomorrow," Ben said.

We finished moving the armoire, and once the couch was installed firmly in the southwest corner, Ben looked at his watch.

"I may be able to still check her out tonight. I'm going to go try."

I made him promise to call me as soon as he found out anything. He kissed me on the forehead, and I melted into a puddle of warm butter right there on the carpet.

THIRTY-SEVEN

THE NEXT MORNING I awoke to twenty more spiders lurking in various predatory spots around my bedroom ceiling. One loomed directly over my head.

"All right, this is war. Get out now or face genocide," I said.

I got dressed and loaded a water bottle, bowl, and some dog cookies into Ernie's Scooby-Doo lunch box. Then I slipped into my brown leather jacket, hooked Ernie's leash to his harness, and jogged with him down the stairs.

A relentless wind coming off the lake blew my hair straight back off my face. Pushed by ferocious blasts, thick clouds and mist sailed toward us from across the water. We hurried to the car.

My Riviera rattled under the gusts as we crossed the bridge on our way to Medication Nation. It was the only place I knew to buy a can of bug spray at seven-thirty on a Sunday morning. In the plaza, I cruised by Estelle's Interior Beauty and BatCave Music. Both were dark. Aside from two cars at the always-open drugstore, the lot was deserted.

"I bet she doesn't have any clients," I told Ernie. "Not one."

Ernie ignored me. He had his front paws on the window-sill and his head out the window. He leaned into the wind and sniffed the misty air, no doubt thinking happy thoughts of flying dachshunds.

I looked at the Medication Nation "Coming Soon" sign. I still had no job. After I got what I needed, I'd do what the sign said and inquire within.

Even though it was only fifty-five degrees, I parked in the shade and left Ernie a bowl of water and a cookie.

I entered through the electric doors and found the household section. They had ten different types of pesticides. I read the labels. This one dissolved nerves, that one melted from the outside in. I looked for which one would be quickest, least painful. I ended up settling on a can of Fatso Ratso Spider Ant and Roach.

At the checkout, I paid for my bug spray and asked the girl about an application. She sent me to the pharmacist at the back of the store.

On the other side of a low wall behind the cash register, the pharmacist placed a prescription bottle in a paper bag and tossed it in a bin. Besides him, the place was deserted.

"Can I have an application, please?"

The pharmacist looked over the wall. He wiped white pill dust on his white pharmacist's smock and walked around his barrier so that he stood behind the cash register.

"Can I help you?

"An application?" I repeated.

"Are you a pharmacist?"

"No."

"Store manager?"

"Um. Maybe?"

He rolled his eyes.

"The store had prescriptions." It was a tropical fish store, but I sometimes gave the sick fish medications.

He sighed and tore an application off a tablet. He handed it to me. "Fill this out. It'll be a big store. If you're not right for management, we'll have plenty of cashier positions."

I watched his back as he walked away, then I sighed. I might have to take a cashier job. And I'd be lucky to be out of jail to take it. At least it was downtown. I filled out the form. He came back, took it from me, and dropped it in a thick file.

"I live downtown," I said. "Where's the store going to be?"

"Between First and Second on Main, east side of the street."

I gasped. "What?" I grabbed onto a condom rack to steady myself. It rocked and tipped over, sending Trojans sliding all over the shiny linoleum. I bent over and started picking up foil packets. I stacked them on the counter.

Only two buildings occupied Main Street between First and Second, the Egyptian and the Acadia Building: Estelle Douglas's Acadia Building. From the floor I said, "First and Main, you're sure?"

He leaned over the counter and looked down. "Yes, we're taking the whole block, so we'll have lots of parking."

"You are not!" I said. I slapped the last condom on the counter and stood up. I stalked through the aisle and out the door.

I stood outside in the wind, clutching my can of Fatso Ratso. I tried to collect my thoughts. I knew everything linked somehow to the Egyptian. I knew it. Now I knew why.

"M.N." stood for Medication Nation. Estelle hired Taz to make sure the Egyptian was in bad shape. She must have known about the notice from a year ago, maybe she'd even planned it.

Why she killed Ronnie, I didn't know. But I was sure, more sure than I'd ever been about anything: she did it.

I walked outside, pulled out my cell, and dialed Ben's number. I got his voice mail. I told him where I was and what I'd just found out, finishing with, "Call me as soon as you get this."

I trotted toward my car. I was almost there when a red Mercedes pulled into the lot and parked in front of Interior Beauty.

I stared at it through the mist—Estelle's red Mercedes—the one we'd almost hit when Ben and I pulled into Medication Nation Plaza the day Taz was killed.

Estelle climbed out of her car. She was dressed for church in a blue silk dress and matching pumps. Her short red hair was moussed into a very messy, jaggedy rat's nest.

I started a silent count to ten. *One . . . two . . . three*—I turned and yelled, "Wait a minute. Wait just a minute." I shoved the bug spray in my pocket and marched over to her.

"We won't quit 'til we're your corner drugstore, huh?" I hollered. "Well, they just quit. And, oh, by the way, I know you killed Taz and Ronnie. You are not getting away with murder."

She turned toward me. "Oh, Kate. I was just going to call you."

I stopped several feet away.

"A trunk's such a handy thing, don't you think?" she said. She clicked her remote. and her hatch levitated silently until the trunk stood open. She flicked a red acrylic nail at it and pointed inside. I stepped closer.

My hands flew to my face. I pressed them against my mouth to stifle a scream. I gulped in air, then hiccupped.

Kitty lay in the trunk. She was dressed in her good, conservative raincoat, the one she saved for church, black with cheetah cuffs. Her limeade hair was tucked under her cheetah turban.

Kitty's neck was bent at an unnatural angle. I couldn't tell if she was out cold or dead.

"We go to the same church, eight o'clock service," Estelle said.

I reached for Kitty. Estelle stepped in front of me, blocking my way.

"You monster!" I shrieked and lunged for her.

She stepped back and ticked one dagger-like nail back and forth like a metronome.

"Naughty, naughty." She pushed the trunk down. "She's still alive . . . I believe. Get in."

I hesitated. I tried to think what to do.

"Come on." She reached in her dress pocket and pulled out a tiny, delicate, pearl-handled pistol.

I got in, and as soon as I did, I smelled gasoline.

She yanked my shoulder bag off my arm and tossed it over the seat. It landed on the floor. Two red plastic containers sat on the blue tarp that covered the seat behind me.

She put the gun in her lap and turned the engine over. She shoved the car in reverse and backed out of the space.

"You should have just left it alone. I was doing you a favor," she said.

The "Wedding March" sounded from the back seat, my cell phone. Estelle ignored it.

"A favor. Really. Ronnie Balfours? Come on, Kate, he didn't have enough money for such a pain in the ass. I'd rather give myself herpes than marry a man like that. What were you thinking? Plus he was weak. When things got a little rough, he choked." She shook her head slowly. "We couldn't have that, could we?" She pulled onto the highway and headed toward Mudd Lake. "And getting you out from under that old dump of a theatre? Those shows are an embarrassment. You should be thanking me. Really. Some people just don't know what's good for them."

"Where are you taking us?" Thoughts raced and whirled through my head. I could jump out. I could grab for the gun. I didn't dare, not with these gas fumes and Kitty stuffed in the trunk. I tried to buy time. "Can I at least see if Kitty's okay?"

"Nosey thing, aren't you?" she said.

The sturdy Mercedes cut through the wind as we crossed the bridge.

"You think you've got Ben Williamson wrapped around your little finger. He came out to see me last night. You've got him digging into things better left alone. Well, no problem, once you're gone, I'll just have to . . . adjust his perspectives."

Her perfect red lips curved into an evil smile. We pulled onto Main Street, then around the corner, behind the Acadia and the Egyptian.

THIRTY-EIGHT

"THESE STREETS ARE SO quiet on Sundays you'd swear this was a ghost town. Tuesday nights are quiet, too."

Estelle smiled again, and the hairs on the back of my neck stood on end.

She pointed her gun at me. "Get out."

I did. Estelle opened the rear door and motioned for me to take the two gas cans.

A shopping cart loaded with bottles, boxes, and an old lamp stood in front of us, beside the Acadia's dumpster. Bunny slippers poked out from behind the lamp.

I raised my voice, projecting, "Estelle, don't do this. Let us go."

I pulled the heavy, sloshing containers out of the back seat. I straightened and looked over Estelle's shoulder. A cottony white head appeared over the lip of the trash bin.

I kept my eyes focused on Estelle. "Don't kill us, please."

Estelle smiled at me, that evil, feline smile. She moved through the misty air to the car. Scottie's head ducked out of sight.

Reaching into my purse, Estelle pulled out my keys. She tossed them to me with her free hand.

"Take those in through the stage door," she said, pointing to the cans.

I unlocked the door, and we stepped into the dark interior back stage.

"I found your golf glove," I said. "Ben's seen it."

"Where are the lights in this rat hole?" she said. "My glove? I had to come back here Tuesday to make sure that idiot Taz hadn't left anything to incriminate me."

I set down the cans and reached for the light switch. Estelle stepped past me, keeping the gun trained on my chest.

The rope to the broken exit door had felt loose that day. Now I knew why. I tried to stall her. "And that's when you dropped your glove?"

"You ask too many questions. I ought to just shoot you on principle, but then, I need a workhorse, don't I?"

She had me carry the cans out front. She followed with the gun pressed between my shoulder blades.

"It wasn't as if I had time to change—Bramblewood Hills, the plaza, here—all in my golf clothes. So inappropriate, but I was running myself ragged."

If she was talking, she wasn't killing, or torching. I asked another question. "Why did you murder Taz?"

"He tried to blackmail me, threatened me with that silly knife. But I had this." She lifted her pistol. "He handed me the knife—stupid, but quite convenient, really, with that trashy girlfriend right next door."

"All this for a drugstore?" I said. She pushed me toward the front row of seats.

"I did it for the town. Once Medication Nation moves in, you'll never know this place. No more tacky theatre, no more tacky Players. Thank God. Medication Nation moves in, and the others will follow." Her eyes glassed over with the vision. "The clothing store chains, home goods stores, they'll all come here. Soon, we'll even be able to get a decent latte." She giggled. "Not you, of course, you'll be cinders." She giggled again. "And, thanks to my pre-nup, with the sale of the Acadia I'll be a rich woman. Correction. Richer woman." She leaned in close. "That's what I really did it for, the money, but I thought I'd impress you with my selfless civic responsibility before I kill you." This time she laughed loudly, a high-pitched sound like breaking glass.

My mind raced around, searching for something I could use as a weapon, some way to stop this insane, greedy, chain-store-crazed killer.

She pushed and prodded me to the front row of seats. "Put the cans right there."

In the wings stood the old wheelchair. Estelle waved the gun toward it.

"Grab that, and we'll get your aunt."

Inside the trunk, Kitty hadn't moved at all. Her neck remained twisted in that unnatural position. I tried to see if she was breathing. I couldn't tell.

Estelle made me pull Kitty from the back of the car and put her limp body in the wheelchair. Kitty's head lolled grotesquely to one side. The shopping cart remained in front of the dumpster. I didn't see Scottie.

I wheeled Kitty through the stage door. The gun poked into the small of my back. Estelle shoved it, jabbing me hard with the barrel.

"Let's move," she said.

I rolled Kitty down the aisle into the auditorium. It was the slightest of movements, almost imperceptible. I looked again to make sure I'd seen it. Kitty twitched her feet. My breathing slowed and became a bit more even. I slid my hand down to Kitty's shoulder and squeezed.

I still hiccupped every thirty seconds, but I didn't care. Kitty was alive.

"Put the wheelchair right there." Estelle waved the gun at the area in front of the orchestra pit.

She pointed to a gas can. "Dowse everything, start with the front row of seats."

I dribbled gas over the first row while she continued to hold the gun on me.

"Estelle, this can't be that important. Why don't you just leave town? Go to Costa Rica, maybe. You'd like it there."

She laughed again, more shattering glass. "Are you kidding? I have stayed the course, through Ronnie's reluctance to condemn this dump, through that idiot Taz, through it all. I even ordered spider eggs on the Internet. Me!"

I trickled gas onto the seat. Estelle came up behind me. She shoved her hand on the gas can forcing it to slosh liquid over the section. "Like this!"

She stepped away. I went back to trickling.

"I thought I'd lost control of him, of Ronnie. I thought I'd give it one more try. You know . . . to convince him to go through with the condemnation. And you caught us. Wasn't that just perfect?" She smiled her feral, feline grin again. "You did it for me."

There had to be something I could do. I searched frantically for an idea. Some weapon I could use.

"Once the theatre burns down and your bodies are nothing but ash, the city will go through with the demolition. They'll take ownership for the cost. Then they'll gladly let this property go for next to nothing. And Medication Nation will buy the whole block, just as I had intended. That albatross, the Acadia Building—it's perfect for the store." She waved her hand around the theatre. "And this for parking."

Behind Estelle, I noticed a slow movement from the wheelchair. Kitty's foot slipped under the tarp. She toed the paintball rifle and slid it across the floor.

Fumes from the gasoline-soaked upholstery rose in visible waves from the front row of seats.

"Do the second row," Estelle said.

I trickled gas across the upholstery.

"Do I have to do everything myself?" Estelle said. She grabbed the remaining gas can and sloshed it over the seats. She soaked the center section of second row.

"Okay, now dowse your aunt," Estelle said.

THIRTY-NINE

"No," I said. I stood where I was, and we locked eyes.

In my peripheral vision, something moved.

Kitty reached down and snatched up the gun. In one swift motion, she pulled it into position and squeezed the trigger. A paint ball shot across the front rows of seats. It hit Estelle in the middle of the back. Estelle slapped at it and whirled around. Yellow paint spread across the back of her blue silk dress.

"I told you I was good!" Kitty crowed.

Estelle raised her pistol, leveling it at Kitty.

I swung the gas can as hard as I could. It smacked the little gun just as it went off. The gun flew from Estelle's hands and sailed across the floor. Estelle and I both lunged for it.

Kitty jumped out of the wheelchair and scrambled toward the gun. It slid under the third row of seats and disappeared.

I sprinted down the second row—Estelle down the third. She dropped down to her knees and felt around under the seat.

I rolled to the floor and put my face to it. I spotted the gun. Estelle almost had her fingers on it.

I stretched my arm under the seats and into the next aisle. My fingertips brushed the gun barrel and pushed it away. I couldn't get a grip on it. Estelle put her face down, too, and we looked at each other under the seats for a split second. I yanked my hand back and shoved it in my jacket pocket. I pulled out my can of Fatso Ratso.

I stuck my face under the seats. "Estelle," I yelped.

Reflexively she rolled her head in my direction as her fingers closed on the gun.

I shoved the can in her face and held the button down. The bug spray shot out and hit her full force in the eyes. I kept spraying.

"Aaaaarrrrrgggggghhhhhh!"

Estelle let go of the gun and clawed at her eyes with both hands. She sputtered, and choked, and rolled over on her back. She writhed on the floor. She reached for the back of a seat and began to pull herself up.

Still wheezing and clutching her eyes, she stood.

"You stupid bitch!" she yelled.

She felt her way to the end of the seats. The gun remained on the floor.

I leapt over a seat and kicked the gun toward Kitty who stood panting at the end of the row. The gun flew about six feet short of her. She scuttled to get it.

I jumped on Estelle's yellow-splotched back and, holding my breath between hiccups, emptied the rest of the can of Fatso Ratso in her face. I yanked my jacket off and threw it over her head. I pulled the sleeves together and knotted them behind her neck.

"Don't move. Don't you dare move," I said.

But she did move. While I'd been spraying Estelle's face, she'd pulled a pack of matches from her pocket. She lit one and held it in the air. Before I could stop her, she tossed it into the puddle of gas on the floor behind us.

There was a whooshing sound, and blue flames rolled down the first two rows.

I heard a sizzling and smelled burning hair. I released my grip on Estelle and jumped out of the way. As flames spread down the seats, I swiveled my head in every direction.

Where was Kitty?

I ran halfway across the theatre, three rows back from the spreading flames. Kitty popped to her feet at the end of the seats. She raced up the aisle toward the door, waving Estelle's gun in the air.

Estelle had ripped my jacket off her head and was sprinting toward the lobby doors from the other side of the seats. She grabbed the handle to the door and jerked it open just as Kitty fired.

A flash lit up the smoky air, and Estelle screamed. She reached both hands behind her and clutched the right cheek of her buttocks. She toppled over sideways onto the carpet and continued to scramble out the door.

"Did you see that, darling?" Kitty hollered. "Just like Annie Oakley."

"The fire's getting bad," I yelled. I coughed and choked on my breath. "Get outside!"

Kitty turned toward me. "Not without you," she yelled. It was hard to see her through the billowing smoke.

Flames leapt across the aisle, blocking off the way to the lobby doors.

"Let it go, Kate. Come on," Kitty called from the doorway.

"No," I screamed. "Get out. I'll be fine!"

At that second I realized saving the theatre wasn't about Kitty. It was about me.

I ran to the wall and pulled the fire alarm, then I yanked the fire extinguisher out of its bracket and pulled the pin. I squeezed the lever. White powder shot from the nozzle. I swept across the licking flames, keeping my aim low. I coated several of the seats, and fire turned to smoke. I moved to the front of the orchestra pit and squirted powdery foam across the front few rows. I squinted through the smoke. My eyes were swelling, and every breath burned my lungs. I hacked and coughed. I pulled my sweater over my nose and mouth and continued to spray.

I worked my way across the front of the theatre and ended up at the side exit. I yanked. It didn't budge. The door held fast. *My bicycle lock.* The flames had subsided, but black billowing smoke continued to pour from the seats. The room was dense with it. Every breath made me cough. I dropped to my knees, put my head to the floor, and inhaled, then I got up to a kneeling position and worked the bicycle lock.

Something moved on the other side of the door, and in a split second I was blinded as the lock flew out of my hands. Two firemen ran past me, and Ben Williamson grabbed my arms and yanked me out the door.

I stood and, with Ben holding my head, hacked until I threatened to cough up both lungs. The same emergency tech who'd worked on Lance last night ran down the alley. He carried a small oxygen tank. He put a mask over my nose and mouth. I breathed in the sweet taste of oxygen, and my thudding heart slowed a bit.

"Fire's out," one of the firemen called through the door. "We're just hosing it down."

"Don't—" I said.

Ben took my hand. "Kate, they have to."

I nodded, the mask still over my nose and mouth.

"We've got Estelle around front. She's not going anywhere. Kitty's okay, too."

"My dog?" I said through the mask. The sun had come out. It didn't take long to kill a dog in a sun-drenched car, even at sixty-five degrees.

"I've got him. I got your message and called your cell. When I didn't get an answer, I drove out to the plaza. I knew you wouldn't leave Ernie in the parking lot, so I figured something must have happened. We got an anonymous 9-1-1 call. It told us Estelle had you here."

I nodded.

"I was with Lance. He woke up this morning," Ben said. "He's going to be all right. Well . . . maybe not all right but . . . alive anyway. You were right. He confessed to robbing old ladies in his birthday suit, nothing more. He never even knew he was suspected of murder."

With one arm around Ben and one around the tech, I walked out of the alley.

I sat on the tailgate of the ambulance watching the firefighters pack up their equipment.

Estelle lay face down on a stretcher in the middle of the sidewalk. Her splotchy yellow dress was hiked up, and a tech busily bandaged her exposed bottom.

She choked and sputtered into the gurney. "I can't breathe," she said. "I can't see." She wheezed and struggled under the straps.

The tech turned to me. "What'd you do to her?"

"Pest control," I said.

"And I shot her," Kitty said. She walked up to us and pulled the pistol out of her raincoat pocket. She wiggled it in the air over her head. Everybody ducked but Estelle, who was already flat on her face.

"Can I keep this?" Kitty asked. She pointed the pistol at the lighthouse tower.

Ben and I both looked at Kitty.

"No!" we barked in unison.

Ben plucked the gun from Kitty's hand. "Evidence," he said. "Sorry."

"Oh. Well, then," she said. She walked over to me. "Are you okay?"

"Yeah," I said. I pulled the oxygen away. I was breathing normally now.

She put her bony arms around me and hugged. "Don't ever do anything that silly again. You hear? It's just a building."

I nodded. "But it's *our* building," I said. "The Players' . . ."

Kitty pulled away and looked me in the eyes. "Kate. It's just a building."

I nodded and hugged her again.

A car pulled up behind the hook and ladder. Two fifty-something men and a woman got out. They all wore suits.

Ben leaned over. "Town council," he whispered.

FORTY

I GROANED AND SHOVED the oxygen mask back over my nose. The woman walked up to one of the firemen. He stood on the back of the truck, folding a hose onto a giant tray.

"We heard about the fire on the scanner and came right over. Can it be saved?" she asked.

"Yeah," he called down, "it's mostly smoke damage and the front two rows of seats. It's not too bad."

"Oh, thank God," the woman said. "We wouldn't want to lose her now, just when we realize what she's worth as a tourist attraction." She turned and gazed up at the Egyptian's marquee.

The oxygen mask kept my jaw from gaping. I took it off and stared at the woman.

She turned to Kitty. "Are you Kitty London? *The* Kitty London?" She pumped Kitty's hand up and down. "I've heard so much about you." She leaned in to Kitty. "Do you mind if I get your autograph? It's for my godson." She pulled a receipt from her purse and flipped it over.

Over the woman's shoulder, Kitty flashed me a thousand kilo-watt smile.

"It's for her godson," she said. She signed her name in big, loopy strokes.

A tall, balding, town council member walked over to where I stood, in front of the tailgate. He waved his hands in the air, surren-der-style. "You win, okay? We voted to make the Egyptian a historic site as of last night. You're safe. Just please, make them stop. We've set up a special e-mail address. Tell people to send 'em there from now on, quit clogging up our system."

"Send what?" I said. I looked from Ben to Kitty. They both shrugged.

"The e-mails," he said. "Damned nuisance is what they are."

The woman said, "Although I must say, hearing from all these movie and theatre stars is very exciting." She looked up at some imaginary image. "I get all fluttery just thinking about it. I didn't even know some of them were still alive."

The other man, short and heavy-set, stepped up beside the first. "We have received over five thousand of the doggone things and counting, from Hollywood, New York, Mudd Lake, and all over the world. They all say the same thing. 'Save the Egyptian, the birth-place of Kitty London's career.' It's driving us nuts."

Kitty's smile, already reaching from ear to ear, stretched to the point that it threatened to swallow her entire face.

I smiled back and wondered if this was all some sort of smoke-induced hallucination.

At that moment, a moped drove up, and Patrice, her hair a glowing shade of hot pink, hopped off.

She ran up to Kitty. "I heard the sirens. Are you guys okay?" She glanced at the Egyptian. "Is it okay?"

Kitty assured her everything was fine. That not only was the fire out, but that the condemnation had been miraculously reversed. The Egyptian was saved.

Patrice nodded. She didn't seem surprised.

I snuck a look at her. She smiled an inscrutable and very toothy smile in my direction.

Ahh.

A state police car pulled up in front of Ben's Tahoe, causing the total count of emergency vehicles on Main Street to exceed the number in the annual Memorial Day parade. Ben excused himself and walked over to their car.

I motioned to Patrice to come close to me. "Look, I can't say I condone what you did."

She looked down. "Yeah, I know. I messed up."

"Yeah, you did." I said. I made my voice stern. This was difficult considering my urge to jump up and down and hug her.

"Yeah, how dumb am I? I should've never sent those e-mails from Bob Hope or Jack Benny. I almost blew the whole thing."

I raised my eyes to the sky and took a deep breath. "That's not what I mean. I'm not sure where the crime is here. Probably something like e-mail fraud. I don't know."

"Nah, there's no crime."

I raised an eyebrow at her.

"Honest. I messed up with the e-mails that looked like they were from the dead guys, but I didn't break any laws. I mean, I didn't sign any names, and all three thousand addresses are legit— mine, or friends of mine. I checked with Charlene first."

I snapped my jaw closed. It was now a habit. "You checked with Char—"

"Yeah, but I made her promise not to tell. Like it's the attorney-client thingy, you know? I didn't want her to spoil the surprise." She wiggled her eyebrows at me, a regular Day-Glo Groucho Marx.

"Did you say three thousand?" I said.

"Yeah." She nodded.

"Town council said they've gotten five thousand e-mails."

"I know. We sent a copy to a few bulletin boards with the Web address and stuff. You know with 'please e-mail these guys'? And we launched the web site. We've been getting tons of hits, fan mail, too." She glanced over at Kitty, who was now signing an autograph for the emergency tech. "People love her."

I shook my head. "You are one amazing kid," I said. "Morally questionable with the fake e-mails, but amazing. Thanks."

I returned the favor by pointing out Taz's killer, bottom up, on the gurney next to us.

All the official vehicles except Ben's pulled away at once, leaving Kitty, Patrice, and me standing on the sidewalk. Ben sat in the Tahoe, talking on his cell phone. I could see Ernie on his lap, sniffing over the edge of the window. Ben petted him while he talked.

We propped all the doors to the theatre wide open and raised the windows to the apartment. Gusts of clean, fall air blew through the building, and the acrid stench of smoke began to dissipate.

"Boy, I had no idea I had so many fans," Kitty told Patrice. "Isn't that something?"

Patrice grinned at her and nodded. "And that's only the beginning. Come on upstairs, and I'll show you your web site." The tongue stud got in the way again, making it come out "webthite."

"My own web site," Kitty said. "Who would've thought it?" If she'd been a lighthouse, her beam could have been seen two Great Lakes away.

Patrice glanced at me. I hesitated for a second, then I nodded. "Go on up," I said. "I'm going to pick up Ernie."

Kitty trailed Patrice up the stairs. "Don't forget to pick up the big one in the tan uniform." She gestured toward Ben. "He's a keeper."

I glanced over at the Tahoe.

"Shhh." I flapped my hands at her. "He'll hear you."

Kitty ignored me. "He's kind of built like a roofer, too." She pointed at her abs. "Twelve pack."

I poked my finger toward the door. "In!" I said.

Patrice and Kitty giggled and disappeared inside.

I walked to the Tahoe and stood beside it. Ernie hopped over to the passenger window and pawed the glass. Ben hung up the phone and reached across the seat, unlatching the door.

I slid in next to him, and Ernie jumped on my lap. He sniffed my singed and smokey hair and began furiously licking my face.

Ben put the car in gear. "LaDonna will be out within the hour. Charges have been filed against Estelle for both murders."

* * *

Ben took the road to the high sandy dunes that overlooked the lake. It was a spot called Exploration Point. And Ben and I had done our share of exploring here, all those years ago.

When we reached the top, he parked, and we sat watching whitecaps far below.

Ben finally spoke. "Do you believe in second chances?"

He held my gaze for a long moment. His eyes were deep blue.

I moved closer to him and tried to slow the pounding of my heart. "They're the only kind of chances I do believe in."

"Me, too," he said. "I need to ask you a question. I want you to think hard before you answer."

My heart did little trampoline bounces. I put Ernie on the floor. I licked my lips and parted them slightly. I wished I had a mint.

Ben took a deep breath, leaned close, and said, "Okay. Here goes. The county's given me approval for a deputy. It's part-time, so you'd have plenty of time for the Egyptian. Do you want the job?"

I snapped my mouth closed.

"Gee, thanks for the offer," I said. I bit the end off the last word.

I swung my head away from him and locked my vision on the last wisps of mist rolling up the coastline. I hadn't murdered a man yet, but at that moment, I came very close.

"Just think about it. You always wanted that tin star. Now you can have a real one."

I kept my eyes fixed on the mist as it curled upward from the water and burned away.

He said, "I've given up on a lot of things over the years. Things that I want back in my life. I'm going back to finish my dental degree. That's why I need the deputy."

"Good for you—leave Mudd Lake behind." I held my voice steady. "Get out while you still can."

"Kate," Ben put his hand on my shoulder. "School's a half hour away—two days a week."

I blinked hard and turned to look at his face.

"I'm not going anywhere," he said.

He kept his hand on my shoulder, then slid it around my back. His lips formed that lopsided smile, and he winked at me.

"And in case you're wondering, that's not the only thing I want back in my life."

ACKNOWLEDGEMENTS:

With a first book there are so many people to thank. I'll try to be brief before I get hooked offstage. Thanks to my wonderful agent Grace Morgan for her faith, encouragement, and hard work. Thanks to my editor Barbara Moore for taking a chance on me. Thanks to Gail, Jason, Lorin, Roman, and the Writers Retreat Workshop family for support, networking, all the great classes, and too much fun. To Jenny Crusie and the Cherries: BTCKE.

Thanks to all my beta readers, including my sister Bonnie, Debbie K., Susan M., Maria B., Doreen O., and of course, my longsuffering little critique group, the Witches: Sharon and Michelle.

For research, I thank Police Chief Gary Goss of Northville, Michigan; Nancy Peska, Executive Secretary of the Community Theatre Association of Michigan; Barbara Gowans, longtime St. Dunstan's Theatre Guild member; John Mogk, Professor of Property Law at Wayne State University; the good folks at the League of Historic American Theatres; and Todd Walsh, State of Michigan Office of Historic Preservation. Any mistakes are my own silly fault—these folks know their stuff.

And I must thank Bobby for keeping my dinner warm and my feet warmer, and Diane, who never once doubted that I could do this.

If you enjoyed reading *Briga-DOOM*
stay tuned for Susan Goodwill's next Kate London Mystery

Little Shop of Murders

coming in March 2008

ONE

"I'll bet Mercury's in retrograde." My Aunt Kitty London's stage whisper echoed through the lobby of Mudd Lake Savings Bank. "This town's crawling with crazy people and drunks."

"The annual Sausage Festival always attracts a weird crowd," I whispered.

"Never do business when Mercury's in retrograde," Kitty said. "That's what Roland says, and he's an excellent astrologer."

Kitty fidgeted from one high-heeled ankle boot to the other and craned her neck around a beefy guy in a *Flaming Sausage* jacket. I craned with her. At the counter, our teller doled twenties into the palm of a well-dressed man with a blond ponytail.

"Kate, this woman is entirely too slow," Kitty said to me, louder this time.

The teller, whose nametag read Chiffon, frowned and arched an eyebrow in our direction. She restarted her count.

I patted Kitty's purple leopard-print sleeve. "Let's just keep a low profile," I whispered.

I eyed my seventy-five-year-old aunt in her faux fur vest, leather mini, and tights—her whole outfit in shades of purple God never put on a grape. Her platinum curls poked out from beneath a tasseled Shriner's fez and dangly purple star earrings reached almost to her shoulders. It'd been forty-odd years since her last movie, but she was the closest thing Mudd Lake had to a celebrity.

Low profile might be asking a lot.

"What if Fred changes his mind?" Kitty's voice went up a notch. "If the planets are out of alignment, Fred could change his mind. Should I call Roland?"

She dug in her fanny pack for her phone.

"Shh! Did you go off decaf again?" I whispered. "Anyway, our loan is approved. Fred said to make our deposits, then to see him and sign the papers."

The planets had better be lined up like billiard balls for this to come off.

Our extremely amateur theatre group, the Mudd Lake Players, had already made it through several surprising hoops—a fundraiser, a decent cast, even renting professional-grade alien plant puppets for the upcoming show.

After the loan, maybe our little dog could jump through that last fiery ring, but it was a doozy. With a disaster-free opening night, we could wow the CracklePops Foundation and get that theatre grant.

A disaster-free opening night.

There's a first time for everything.

I glanced around for Fred Schnebbly, the banker who held the London family's fate in his pencil-pushing hands. His office sat dark and unoccupied.

Kitty zoomed in on the other, more familiar face behind the counter: Patrice Stikowski. Patrice counted stacked bills behind a "Next Window" sign.

Kitty hoisted her tote bag high. "Halloo, Patrice!" she trilled. "Be a dear and wait on us. I've got five thousand dollars from the theatre benefit. It's making me quite nervous. Plus, Kate's got all the town's cash from the Sausage Festival." She jerked a thumb at my satchel.

I ran a hand through my auburn curls, gazed at the high ceiling, and sighed.

"Is that okay?" Patrice sent a questioning look over to Chiffon. The spring sunlight glinted off two new eyebrow rings, and Patrice's hair, a conservative new-bank-teller-black, made her look like a Goth Snow White. "Can I open up?"

"You're not to open until Rhonda gets in." Chiffon huffed and slapped a stack of twenties on the counter. "I can't imagine where that girl has gotten to."

Patrice was Kitty's biggest fan and until recently, Kitty's only fan without an AARP card.

I sent Patrice a grin. "Thanks for trying."

"We theatre people have to stick together, you know?" Stick came out "thtick" around her tongue stud.

Kitty reached in her bag and pulled out a rolled up poster. She unfurled it to reveal a cartoon picture of a giant, snaggle-toothed, man-eating-alien-plant. Underneath, the words "*Little Shop of Horrors*, opening May 25th, at Mudd Lake's historic Egyptian Theatre" seemed to drip blood.

Kitty waved the poster at Chiffon. "Might we put this in the win—"

The door behind us whacked against the wall, and we all jumped. A whoosh of breezy Lake Michigan air blew past us, and a stooped, balding man in a red plaid bathrobe and floppy slippers burst into the lobby. He scuttled to the counter.

I guessed him to be about eighty years old. I smiled and leaned toward Kitty. "Sausage Festival fallout."

The geezer slipped around the ponytailed man at the front of our line. He swiveled toward us and shoved his hand in his bathrobe pocket. An outline of something jabbed out through the flannel.

My smile evaporated, and my heart slammed against my ribcage. A gun?

My throat tightened, and I grabbed Kitty's hand and squeezed.

"Everybody keep calm," the old man rasped. He hacked phlegm from his throat and swiveled to Chiffon. He pulled a crumpled IGA bag from his left bathrobe pocket and kept his other pocket low, below the counter. "This is a hold-up."

Chiffon flicked a curtain of beaded cornrows over her shoulder and put one fist on her hip. She shoved the grocery bag back toward the old man and wagged a very long, very fake, green and white fingernail at him. "We're too busy for this today, Walter."

The elderly man took his hand from his pocket and cupped it to his ear. "Eh?"

The teller leaned over and raised her voice. "Did you get a new prescription or something?"

"What the-?" He stomped a floppy-slippered foot. "Dang it, Chiffon, of all the times to be a pain in the butt, this ain't it. Do what I say!"

"Nuh-uh. You go on home." She brushed her hand at him. "Shoo!"

He shifted his frail frame and planted his hands on his hips. Chiffon grabbed a chocolate frosted doughnut from a Krispy Kreme box behind the counter and chomped off a hunk. She glared at Walter while she chewed. The two spent several long seconds locked in a standoff. No one in the bank moved.

Frozen in place, I stared at the gun-shaped object that sagged in Walter's pocket. I poked my head up to make contact with Chiffon. I tried pointing to the pocket with my eyeballs.

No response.

I jerked my head in the pocket's direction. I stretched my eyelids wide and mouthed the word "gun."

Chiffon looked over the robber's shoulder and frowned. "You got a problem?"

The old man spun around, shoved his hand back in his pocket, and glared at us. I snapped my jaw shut and made my face a blank. My grip tightened on Kitty's hand.

"It'll be okay," Kitty whispered, her voice very quiet.

The old man looked at Kitty, then at me. He turned back to Chiffon. Out of the corner of my eye, I watched Patrice ease her hand toward the edge of the counter. Walter swished his pocket into view, exposing blue-and-white-striped pajama bottoms. He pointed his pocket at the scabby double rings in Patrice's newly-pierced left eyebrow.

"You! Away from the alarm. You want another hole in your fool head?"

Patrice let her hand fall and swallowed hard. Chiffon's eyes grew large. The last of her doughnut dropped to the floor.

"He's got a gun? He's got a gun? He's never got a gun." She stuck her arms in the air. "Help!"

Keeping his pocket pointed at Chiffon, Walter pushed the grocery bag back across the metal counter. Mudd Lake is a small town and I'd never noticed until now, our teller windows were wide open. No bulletproof glass.

"Give me all your twenties," he said.

I hiccupped.

Uh-oh," Kitty whispered. "Try holding your breath."

Hic.

"It doesn't help," I said.

"I know," she whispered. "How're you going to be a law enforcement official, if you get the hiccups all the time when you're scared?"

"Shhh," I said and hiccupped again.

The man with the ponytail moved closer to Walter.

"And you," Walter spun around and shoved his gun pocket into the man's chest. "Back off!"

Walter snatched the wad of cash from the ponytailed man's fist. Startled, the man's empty hand hung in the air for several seconds before he dropped it to his side.

Chiffon dug in her cash drawer. She grabbed banded stacks of twenty-dollar bills and dropped them into the bag.

Walter swiveled to Patrice.

"I want all your twenties. Every one of 'em!"

While Patrice emptied her drawer, the old man looked around nervously. Kitty lifted her free arm and wiggled her fingers in a wave.

I hiccupped and jerked her hand. I clutched the satchel full of the town's money and tried not to move my lips.

"Don't draw attention to us," I whispered.

Too late.

The robber squinted at Kitty. He flashed a mouth full of over-sized dentures in our direction and pulled his gun hand out of his pocket. He wiggled his fingers back.

Kitty smiled tentatively. I tried not to roll my eyes. Kitty'd had seven husbands for a reason. She was a hopeless flirt.

The bandit's attention moved from Kitty to the swarthy guy in the Flaming Sausage jacket.

The man in the jacket stepped closer to Kitty and put a meaty hand on her shoulder. In a thick Greek accent he said, "Hey buddy, we want no troubles. Just do your job."

Walter squinted at him, then rammed his hand back in his pocket and whirled. He swooped his gun-pocket at Patrice. "Hurry the hell up!"

Patrice tossed her stack of bills to Chiffon. Chiffon loaded them in the paper bag and slid it across the counter to Walter. The old man snatched it and headed for the door. He stopped in front of us.

I clutched Kitty's hand, pressed the satchel to my side, and hiccupped.

"What's in those bags?" he said. He took a step forward.

Kitty jutted her chin and squeezed her tote bag to her chest. I moved in front of her.

"You ladies got cash?" Walter wrapped bony fingers around the strap of my satchel.

My heart slapped a rhythmic message in my ribcage. *Do something, do something.* I thought of that gun, the people around us, Kitty right beside me. A sinking feeling took over, and I let him pull the satchel from my grasp.

He peered at Kitty. "Hey Kitty, is that the theatre money?"

"None of your beeswax, Walter," she said.

"Let him have it," I whispered and hiccupped.

Kitty stepped around me and whipped the bag in a wide arch. She walloped Walter full in the head with five thousand dollars in tens, twenties, and miscellaneous loose change.

"Aack!" Walter staggered back a step. He grabbed for his head with both hands, and a banana flew out of his bathrobe pocket.

A banana?

My breath escaped in a whoosh, and I lunged.

Walter rocked backward, took another step to steady himself, and stepped on the banana. It squished out of its skin and sailed past my left ankle.

Walter leapt at Kitty and tugged her tote bag free. Kitty pitched forward, going in like the world's most diminutive, platinum-haired quarterback on a loose ball.

A flash of Kitty with a broken hip blazed before me. I thrust out my arm and snatched a fistful of purple faux-bunny. Keeping a tight hold, I grabbed for the bags with my free hand. Walter jerked backward, circled around us, and setting some sort of old-fart-in-pajamas land speed record, sprinted to the exit.

I let go of Kitty, and she hotfooted it across the lobby.

The guy in the sausage jacket, the ponytailed man, and I all bolted for the door. Kitty got there first. She stood in the doorway.

"Walter, you're a rat's patootie!" she hollered.

A flash of plaid flannel disappeared around the corner one building away.

"You know that guy?" I said, staring after it.

"You bet I do, the jackass!" Kitty said. "I'm dating him."

TWO

"What?" I gaped at Kitty.

Tires screeched. A late model blue Taurus careened around the corner; its windows mirrored with sunshine—its plates caked with mud.

"You heard me."

Kitty was halfway to her car, a mammoth white 1974 Eldorado convertible with red leather interior, a.k.a. the Land Yacht. I caught up and clutched her shoulder.

"Wait! We can't leave. The police'll be here any minute." I took a deep breath of the blustery Lake Michigan air and eased it out. "You're dating him?"

"Walter's a fabulous Salsa dancer, but I'm breaking up with him as soon as we get our loot back. I'm hopping mad. Let's go."

Kitty shrugged me off and crossed a strip of grass to the car. She grabbed the handle on the passenger side and yanked the huge door open.

I hesitated and listened for a siren. Nothing.

"We've got to catch him," Kitty said. "He has our theatre money and by Godfreys, we're getting it back."

"Kitty, it's too dangerous."

"You drive," she said. "When I'm upset, I get the gas and brake mixed up."

Adrenaline fizzled through my veins and my thoughts raced: Sheriff Ben Williamson had trusted me with the Sausage Festival deposit. Then there was the benefit money—with the loan, the Egyptian's ticket to respectability.

I stood at the driver's door. I yanked it open and hopped inside. "Let's go."

Kitty tossed me the keys. "To think I almost went Viagra shopping with that man."

My eyes squeezed shut against the image. I popped them open and shoved the key in the ignition. "You really know this guy."

"Everybody knows him," Kitty said. She smoothed a tuft of errant purple fur. "He's Fred Schnebbly's uncle."

I revved the engine. "He just robbed his own nephew's bank?"

Kitty just sat there steaming.

I executed a complicated five-point u-turn and tried to think like a crook.

I pressed the big accelerator pedal and flew over the three blocks to the bypass highway. We roared down the entrance ramp and headed south toward Detroit—more traffic to blend in with that way—more criminals. The highway was empty but for two semis in the distance. I jammed my foot to the floor. The tires screeched and swallowed pavement. The thin accelerator needle slid across the big white numbers until the engine jolted us into high gear around sixty or sixty-five. We whizzed past the two startled semi drivers.

"Wow!" Kitty yelled over the howling engine, "Just like Thelma and Louise!"

"Excuse me, but they died in that car!" I hollered.

"Details." Kitty flapped a hand at me and squinted at the highway.

Somewhere around ninety-five miles an hour I spotted the Taurus. It crested the hill a quarter mile or so in front of us. We were closing fast.

"Is that him?" Kitty asked.

"Yep," I said. I blew the horn and flashed the lights. "Grab my phone and call Ben."

Along with being Mudd Lake's sheriff, Ben Williamson is my on-again off-again boyfriend.

Kitty undid her seatbelt and twisted her torso. She reached over the back seat.

I shot her a look expecting to see my cell phone. Instead Kitty hoisted an odd-looking rifle into her lap. I let out a gasp and shrieked. "What the—? What are you doing? Are you crazy? Put that thing down!"

I swatted in Kitty's direction. We fishtailed into the next lane. Clutching the big steering wheel with both hands, I pulled us back on course. I eased off the gas, and the Taurus racked up several car lengths on us.

"You can't just shoot him!" I looked again at the gun. "Is that the paintball gun? From the Egyptian?"

Kitty shoved the gun barrel out her window. "Don't get your panties in a pretzel, darling. I simply want to scare him so that he pulls over."

Kitty yanked off her fez and stuck her head into the howling wind. Her hair whipped around her eyes, and she pushed it out of the way.

"I played a stellar Annie Oakley," she yelled over the roaring engine.

The Taurus now had six or seven car lengths and counting.

Kitty pulled her head back in. "Kate, he's getting away! Floor it!"

"Don't fire that thing, okay?" I took a deep breath and muttered, "I'm an idiot."

Then I punched it. The fierce seventies motor howled, and we swallowed the gap to three car lengths. Then two.

I cut to the other lane, pulled beside Walter's car, and blew the horn. Walter's startled face appeared pressed against the rear driver's window. I glanced at him. Had he mouthed the word "help"? I couldn't be sure. He might've been hacking phlegm.

"Uh-oh," Kitty said. She pulled the rifle to her lap and sent her window up. "Did I just conspire to assassinate a president?"

I glanced over at the car and blinked. From the driver's seat, former U.S. President and cigar aficionado William Jefferson Clinton looked back. He didn't blink.

"That's a mask," I said.

"Phew. Scared me for a second." Kitty said, patting her windblown hair.

I let off the gas, and the car gained distance on us. The gap grew back to six car lengths.

"Mask or no mask," I eyed the big man behind the wheel, "we don't want to mess with Bill."

ABOUT THE AUTHOR

Susan Goodwill has been involved in many aspects of community theatre from popping popcorn to wielding power tools. She's ushered guests, swept the stage, even taken out the trash. In fact, she's done just about anything possible for a theatre person with stage fright.

Prior to a successful career selling telecommunications, she created stage clothes for rock bands, among them Electric Light Orchestra and Bob Seger and the Silver Bullet Band.

She is a graduate of the prestigious Writers Retreat Workshop and a member of Sisters in Crime, Mystery Writers of America, American Mensa, and Jenny Crusie's Cherries. *Briga-DOOM* is her first novel.

Susan lives in a 1927 cottage-style home on a small lake in Michigan with her human and rescued-dog family. She is busy finishing the second book in the Kate London Mystery Series, *Little Shop of Murders.*

WWW.MIDNIGHTINKBOOKS.COM

From the gritty streets of New York City to sacred tombs in the Middle East, it's always midnight somewhere. Join us online at any hour for fresh new voices in mystery fiction, book club questions, author information, mystery resources, and more.

Midnight Ink promises a wild ride filled with cunning villains, conflicted heroes, hilarious hazards, mind-bending puzzles, and enough twists and turns to keep readers on the edge of their seats.

MIDNIGHT INK ORDERING INFORMATION

Order by Phone:

- Call toll-free within the U.S. and Canada at
  1-888-NITEINK (1-888-648-3465)
  - We accept VISA, MasterCard, and American Express

Order by Mail:

Send the full price of your order (MNresidents add 6.5% sales tax) in U.S. funds, plus postage & handling to:

Midnight Ink
2143 Wooddale Drive
Woodbury, MN 55125-2989

Postage & Handling:

Standard (U.S., Mexico, & Canada). If your order is:
$24.99 and under, add $3.00
$25.00 and over, FREE STANDARD SHIPPING

AK, HI, PR: $15.00 for one book plus $1.00 for each additional book.

International Orders (airmail only):
$16.00 for one book plus $3.00 for each additional book

Orders are processed within 2 business days. Please allow for normal shipping time.
Postage and handling rates subject to change.